Drifter's Revenge

They called him Drifter, because that's what he'd done most of his life. But no matter where he went, he always came back to Santa Rosa, New Mexico – the nearest thing he had to a home.

Still, there was trouble brewing outside town, and though Drifter wanted no part of it, fate had other ideas. Against his better judgment he signed on to help a sodbuster named Albright . . . and when the time came, he took Albright's side against Stillman J. Stadtlander, the ruthless cattle baron who was determined to claim Albright's land for himself.

Drifter should have saddled up and made dust, but that wasn't his way. Besides . . . there was Albright's wife, Hannah, and her daughter, Lydon, to think about. And though he tried to resist his feelings for them, they still stole his heart. So he loaded his guns and stepped out to challenge Stillman's rawhiders . . . and that's when hell broke loose.

Drifter's Revenge

Steve Hayes

A Black Horse Western

ROBERT HALE

© Steve Hayes 2020
First published in Great Britain 2020

ISBN 978-0-7198-3069-3

The Crowood Press
The Stable Block
Crowood Lane
Ramsbury
Marlborough
Wiltshire SN8 2HR

www.bhwesterns.com

Robert Hale is an imprint
of The Crowood Press

The right of Steve Hayes to be identified as
author of this work has been asserted by him
in accordance with the Copyright, Designs and
Patents Act 1988

Dedication
To my 'gym rat' friends, C.J. And Chad

Typeset by
Derek Doyle & Associates, Shaw Heath
Printed and bound in Great Britain by
4Bind Ltd, Stevenage, SG1 2XT

CHAPTER ONE

It had been a long, hot, dusty ride from Silver City to Santa Rosa, New Mexico. But now that the sun had sunk behind the San Cristobal Mountains, bringing a much welcomed dusk, it had grown cooler and Quint Longley, an aging gunfighter known throughout the southwest as Drifter, gratefully reined up his tired, sweat-caked sorrel outside Gustafson's Livery Stable on Front Street.

The stable's big barn-like doors were open, and inside an old lantern hanging from the rafters cast long, eerie shadows over the unsaddled horses feeding in the stalls. Drifter couldn't see anyone, but he could hear a man humming 'The Old Chisholm Trail' as he swept up the urine-soaked straw covering the floor in back.

Knowing that the cheerful ditty was not only Lars Gustafson's favorite song but a signal to the ever-cautious Drifter that it was safe to enter, he relaxed, took his hand from his holstered pistol and smiled, pleased by the thought of seeing his old and trusted friend.

Suddenly the sorrel snorted and impatiently stamped the ground with its foreleg, as if to remind Drifter that it, too, was tired, hungry and thirsty.

'Yeah, yeah, I hear you,' Drifter grumbled. 'Don't go off half-cocked on me. Remember, caution's the way.' It was his favorite phrase and it usually spurred him into thoughtful action. But not this time. He was too damned tired. He still didn't move. His mind told him to step down, but his body was too exhausted to respond. He remained in the saddle, slumped over the weary stallion's neck, trying to gather the strength to dismount.

As he sat there, Drifter heard the familiar tinkling of an upright piano coming from the Copper Palace on Lower Front Street. The thought of the popular saloon, one of Santa Rosa's original buildings that was run by Roy O'Halloran and his crew of cheerful Irish bartenders – Dubliners all, famous throughout the southwest for their shamrock-green shirts, starched white collars, green-and-white polka-dotted bow ties and large, wax-tipped handlebar mustaches – reminded Drifter how thirsty he was.

He was so thirsty in fact that he momentarily toyed with the idea of riding over to the Palace before stabling his weary horse. But it had taken them four sweltering days and five bone-chilling cold nights to cross the vast barren desert, and during that time both he and the sorrel had been forced to limit themselves to a few tepid, metal-tasting sips of water that Drifter had eked out of his leaky canteen.

As a result, he knew that in his dehydrated condition one or two drinks wouldn't satisfy his thirst;

instead, they would just lead to another, and then another, until he was sufficiently pie-eyed to forget all about stabling his horse – which would not only be selfish, but could prove to be a fatal mistake. Because as Drifter well knew, there were times when he relied on the sorrel's speed and stamina to outrun pursuers, whether it was a posse after him for an old misdeed or the kin of some swaggering would-be gunman trying to enhance his reputation by gunning down a famous shootist.

Drifter always tried to talk them out of a show-down, but was seldom successful. Bolstered by their false bravado, the cocky young guns mistook his reluctance to draw as a sign of cowardice, and only grew bolder and more threatening ... until finally Drifter had no choice but to shoot them. Their death gave him no pleasure. Quite the opposite. With each shooting his conscience grew heavier. And as the number of killings mounted over the years, and his reputation grew, he found himself withdrawing further and further from society until he eventually became the consummate loner, a solitary drifter who only took on ranch work when he needed eating money.

Tonight, however, wasn't one of those times. Thanks to several winning hands during a five-card draw poker game in Silver City, Drifter was flush. But he was also ever-cautious. And earlier, when he'd ridden into town, he had decided that rather than risk running into any trigger-happy gunmen or bounty hunters in the old, bawdy Copper Palace, for the time being he would put his desire for whiskey or tequila on hold and play it safe. So reluctantly, he had urged on his weary sorrel along Front Street to the livery stable.

CHAPTER TWO

Now, as Drifter prepared to dismount, Lars Gustafson's gravelly voice came from the rear of the lantern-lit, dung-smelling livery stable.

'You know, bucko, it'd be a mite easier on that pony of yours if you was to step down from that saddle.'

If Drifter heard the stableman, his bleak, almost sour expression didn't show it.

'Be a hell-sight easier on me, too . . .'

Drifter again ignored the old stableman.

'Because once you step down, bucko, I can go about my business and get the sorrel stalled and grained. Then I can tend to my supper and afterwards, maybe, *just maybe* even steal me a few winks of shuteye, which I could most sorely use.'

Drifter still showed no sign of hearing Lars. He sat rock-still, his trail-raw gray eyes staring straight ahead as if he were trying to see the future. But in fact, it was the past that he was revisiting.

One night during the long ride, he'd lost his black, flat-crowned hat in a swirling dust storm. He'd searched long and hard for it without success, and eventually he'd been forced to give up. As a result, his leathery skin and long shaggy black hair were caked with dirt. But though he longed for a hot bath, dirt wasn't the reason for his sour disposition. It was the loss of his hat. His daughter, Deputy US Marshal Liberty Mercer, had given it to him on his forty-fifth birthday, and he'd treasured it ever since. Consequently, losing it had cut deep and Drifter, normally a quiet, hard-to-rile man, was now on the prod.

'Maybe I ain't figuring on stepping down,' he growled. 'Ever consider that?'

'Nope.'

'Why in hell not?'

' 'Cause if that was your intention, bucko, you wouldn't've brung that wore-out pony here in the first place.'

'I didn't "brung" him nowhere. Ugly son-of-a-buck brung hisself.'

'And you – you just happened to hump along for the ride. That your story?'

'Close.'

'Birds of a feather.'

'Meaning?'

'Just remembering something this drifter I once knew told me . . .' Lars broke off in a fit of coughing, then added hoarsely: 'Said, close only counts in horseshoes.'

'And Ketchum grenades.'

'Ah, there you got me, bucko. I was too crippled to fight in Mr Lincoln's war, so I reckon I'll just have to take your word for it.'

'It ain't a word given lightly.'

10

'So I've heard.'

'Maybe you also heard how that same "drifter" don't take kindly to being prodded.'

'Now you mention it, seems like that did crop up during our powwow. That, and how these days integrity was harder to find than gold up a duck's ass!'

Drifter hid a smile and rubbed his nose with his fist, a habit he'd acquired while growing up in a Santa Fe orphanage. 'Sounds about right. Did he also happen to mention how he didn't take kindly to sarcasm – especially from his pals?'

'More than once, if I recall correctly. But you see . . .' Lars again broke off in a fit of coughing that sprayed blood-flecked spittle everywhere '. . . there's the rub.'

'Meaning?'

'Well, no offense meant, but you could count the number of this drifter's pals on one hand and still have five fingers left over. So, sarcasm wasn't never an issue.'

'Fair enough . . .' Drifter gave a rare smile and his mood softened. 'Well, since you seem curious as to why I'm here, the truth is – a few miles back on the trail, I gave the sorrel his head and nodded off. I only figured on taking a catnap, but when it comes to sleeping, hell, nothing beats a gently rocking saddle and when I next opened my eyes, here I was, outside your stable on a wore-out horse.'

There was no answer. Just the sound of coughing – an ugly, death-rattling cough that seemed to last forever. When it finally stopped, Drifter heard limping footsteps approaching. A moment later Lars

11

Gustafson appeared from in back. A hunched-over, balding Swede with a stubbly salt-and-pepper beard and a toothless grin, he was crippled by arthritis and had to cling to a pitchfork in order to walk. But despite his painful ailments, a more cheerful man didn't exist.

'Talking of wore-out horses,' he chided, 'when'd you last have a sit-down with your conscience?'

'Meaning?'

'Well, it's bad enough that you damn' nigh rode the sorrel's legs off. Do you now got to keep a-warming that saddle till the exhausted critter dies under you?'

'What's so bad about dying?'

'Reckon only the dead can answer that.'

'Or a man who deals in lead.' As if to prove his point, Drifter's right hand moved with blurring speed and his Dragoon Colt .44 appeared almost magically in his fist. He thumbed back the hammer and rested the long-barrelled, single-action pistol atop the saddle horn.

Lars was too busy coughing to notice – or care. Clinging to the pitchfork, he stood hunched over, hacking away. His coughing brought up more blood-flecked saliva, indicating that he hadn't long to live. But even that daunting prospect didn't dim his inde-fatigable spirit. What the hell, he'd joke when asked about his poor health, nobody rides the high lines forever. And since at sixty-one Lars had already out-lived all the original settlers in Santa Rosa, he figured he had nothing to bitch about.

Now, unfazed by his imminent death, Lars waited for the coughing to stop, then spat out an oyster the size of a silver dollar. He then straightened up, took a plug of Copenhagen from his pocket, bit off half and tossed the other half to Drifter.

The tall, whip-lean, slab-shouldered gunfighter whose hawkish face was darkly tanned from a life in the saddle, deftly caught the wad of chewing tobacco with his left hand and slipped it in his mouth. He then transferred the wad with his tongue into his right cheek and nodded his thanks.

Lars wiped the bloody spittle from his bearded lips before saying reflectively: 'Come to think of it, bucko, this ain't the worst place your pony could've brung you.'

'It ain't?'

'Uh-uh. Remember that "drifter" I just told you about? Well, he mentioned that one time he nodded off in the saddle and when he next come awake, his horse had ridden him straight to hell.'

'Interesting. How'd he cope with that?'

'Faced down the devil, from what I hear.'

'Then what happened?'

'No one knows. He vanished faster than a shadow at dusk.'

'Go on.'

'Nothing more to tell. Ever since then, it's like he never even existed.'

'Hell, that makes me feel better already.'

Lars chuckled. 'All funning aside, bucko, I got me a pot of hot coffee in back that's just itching to rot out some fella's gut.'

'Finally got that old stove of yours working, huh?'

'I wish.'

13

'Then how'd you boil the coffee?'

'I didn't. I got Lonnie Forbes to thank for it. He kindly brung the pot by after he got through mooching a free dinner at the Carlisle Hotel.'

Drifter grunted disgustedly, rubbed his nose with his fist and in one blurringly swift, fluid motion holstered his pistol. He'd always had unnaturally fast reflexes. And back in '85, when he'd bought the gun, he'd helped quicken his draw by filing off the front sight, making the long-barreled pistol easier and smoother to yank from his tied-down holster. He'd also diligently practised drawing and shooting the weapon from the hip until he got so accustomed to its weight, balance and the sensitive pull of its hairtrigger, the pistol became an integral part of his hand. As a result, on those occasions when he was forced into a shootout, Drifter no longer had to think about drawing his gun but did it instinctively, eventually becoming so fast that he became legendary.

Many folks who'd witnessed his gunfights claimed he was the fastest gun in the territory, which was high praise indeed considering that his contemporaries were Billy the Kid, John Wesley Hardin and James 'Wild Bill' Hickok.

But Drifter was too pragmatic to be impressed by accolades. He knew that no matter how fast he could draw, a bullet in the back would kill him just as quickly as anyone else – which is why he lived each day as if it was his last.

'You know,' he now grumbled to Lars, 'this may come as a surprise, *compadre*, but there are times when

I can't throw a rope over you.'

The old stableman chuckled. 'You mean, like now, for instance?'

When Drifter didn't reply, Lars cocked his bald head, vulture-like, and critically eyed the tall, broad-shouldered gunfighter. 'Look, if something's gnawing at you, bucko, spit it out, 'cause right now I ain't catching your drift.'

'Fair enough, amigo. Then I'll get straight to the meat: what's bothering me is how you – one of the few *hombres* I respect – has gotten so damned cozy with that no-good, lump-headed weasel wearing a tin star! I mean, if that ain't a friendship made in hell, I don't know what is.'

Lars made a face. 'Aww, c'mon, Quint! Lonnie's got his faults, same as the rest of us, but he ain't so bad. Not once you get to know him.'

'Neither was Adam – till he gave Eve that apple to eat.'

'Eve gave it to Adam, you dumb heathen! Got your Bible ass-backwards, like most everything else in your miserable wandering life!'

'Maybe so. But at least I know which side of the law I'm on – which is more than that chiseling sidewinder Lonnie Forbes does!'

'Wrong again. Lonnie knows. But he also knows who put him in office. So, when Old Man Stadtlander says jump, Lonnie's only answer is: "How high?"'

'That go for you, too?'

'Me and everyone else in business around here, sure.'

'Groveling?' Drifter spat disgustedly into the hay.

'May as well sell your soul to the devil while you're at it.'

'Mean, like *you* done, Mister-Quint-Longley?'

Drifter flinched and his gray eyes hardened, but he didn't duck the accusation. 'Yeah. Like I done.'

'Any regrets?'

'None.'

'None?'

'Nope. See, the way I figure it, regretting something you said or done ain't only hypocritical, it's a pure waste of time. It's like saying you're sorry. Words don't change nothing and, worse, they make a fella sound like he's whining.'

'Don't complain, don't explain, that it?'

It was another of Drifter's favorite sayings and he growled: 'Got that right.'

'Just slap leather faster than the next fella?'

'Right, again, *compadre.*'

'Some philosophy that is!'

'Yeah, and don't think I ain't been paying the devil's piper for it ever since.'

'Drifting?' Lars shrugged. 'That don't seem like much of a punishment to me.'

'Talking from years of experience, are you?'

'OK, so I ain't wore out too many saddles. But I'll tell you this, bucko – and this is from years of experience – no matter how bad drifting is, it can't be no worse than shoveling piss-wet hay or stinking prairie pancakes out of this hell hole every day!'

'You could always move on, *compadre.* Santa Rosa ain't the only cow town in the territory.'

'It is for me. I'm too old and crippled to pick up

16

stakes and start again.'

'So, this is trail's end for you?'

'I reckon.'

'Hell, I never figured I'd live long enough to hear you admit defeat.'

'I ain't defeated, damn it. Just resigned to my fate, is all.'

'There's a difference?'

'Damn' straight!' Lars broke off, hacked up another oyster and spat it into the hay. 'Now, if you're all done preaching, bucko, how about climbing down from your pulpit and enjoying some of my coffee? It ain't strong enough to straighten out your short-and-curlies, but I promise you this, a cup or two will surely chase the dust from your mouth.'

'Fair enough, *amigo*.' Drifter dismounted and handed Lars the reins. As he did, his sorrel, ornery as ever, swung his head around and tried to bite him. But Drifter, anticipating it, jumped back and cursed the leggy, flaxen-maned horse.

Lars gave a toothless grin. 'Still as sweet-tempered as ever, I see.'

'Does Lucifer have horns?'

'Reckon I'll be finding out soon enough . . .' Lars broke off, coughed violently then spat out more blood-speckled mucus '. . . when the Good Lord calls on me.'

'Trust me, *compadre*, that won't be for quite a spell.'

'Really? Got that straight from the Man Upstairs, did you?'

'Nope. But the way I figure it, since He knows you lead the church choir on Sundays and always put

17

money in the collection box, I can't see Him calling on you anytime soon.'

Lars chuckled wryly. 'I hope you're right, bucko, 'cause I ain't ready to call it quits yet.' Limping along with the help of the pitchfork, he led the exhausted, ill-tempered sorrel to an empty stall. 'Meanwhile, let's me and you do what we do best: chew the fat and swap lies about how good life's treating us.'

'Best offer I've had today,' Drifter said, ' 'specially if you got a slug of red-eye to punch up that coffee, *compadre*.'

'Bottle's in the rain barrel . . . same as always.'

CHAPTER THREE

Later that evening, after the two old friends had drained the last drop of whiskey from the bottle, Drifter left the livery stable, crossed the wind-swept street and headed for Melvin's Mercantile & Haberdashery Store to buy a hat, a canteen and a box of shells for the well-oiled 45-70 Winchester '86 that he always carried.

The wind had gotten worse. The swirling dust forced folks to hold on to their hats, turn up their collars and squint as they trudged along the board-walk. Sadly, in their eagerness to reach their destination, they ignored what was taking place in the alley beside the store. There, a pretty, tawny-haired teenager named Lydon Albright was struggling to fight off three men who had her pinned against the wall while they groped her and smothered her with slobbering kisses.

Drifter would have liked to have ignored her, too. But weary and thirsty as he was, his conscience wouldn't let him. Being a man meant being responsible. And

Drifter, having lived by that code all his adult life, had no choice but to help her. And though he didn't know who she was, he did know two of her attackers from past run-ins with them. They were the Iverson brothers, Mace and Cody, and Drifter, like most of the townspeople, had no use for them.

As for the third man, a small, lithe gunslinger named Clay Hudson, Drifter had heard tell of him, but never had any dealings with him. But from all accounts, he was mad-dog mean and enjoyed killing.

No one would have suspected it, though. Not by looking at him. Unlike the Iverson brothers, who reveled in their disheveled appearance and disreputable persona, Clay was fastidiously neat and tidy and had the manners of a gentile southern gentleman. Dressed all in gray, he wore a tailored jacket over a stylish velvet waistcoat with mother-of-pearl buttons, soft leather gloves and expensive hand-tooled boots with elevator heels that made him taller than his natural five feet three inches. He was effeminately handsome with fine, delicate features, ice-blue eyes and a thin-lipped sneering smile that personified cruelty. Long golden curls hung from under his immaculate high-crowned Stetson, reaching all the way to his narrow shoulders, while on his hips two fancy ivory-handled, nickel-plated Colt .45s were tucked into tied-down, fast-draw holsters that were adorned with shiny silver Mexican centavos.

Drifter summed up the gunman in a single glance, immediately noticing that Clay's left holster was a little more worn than the right, indicating he was a natural lefty. Drifter stored the knowledge away in case he ever needed it, and then turned his attention to the Iversons.

The brothers were known bullies and troublemakers, and Drifter, blood boiling, relished the chance to humiliate them. Approaching from behind, he slammed his rifle butt against the back of Mace's head. Momentarily stunned, Mace stumbled forward and almost dropped to his knees. But somehow, he managed to keep his feet and angrily spun around, reaching for his six-gun, ready to shoot his attacker.

'Go ahead,' Drifter goaded as Mace, on recognizing the aging gunfighter, hesitated to draw. 'There ain't nothing I'd like better than to gun you down right here and now – you *and* your cowardly, pig-swilling brother!'

Mace whitened with rage. But too afraid to challenge Drifter, he made no attempt to slap leather. Beside him, his brother Cody and Clay Hudson stopped molesting Lydon and turned to face Drifter.

'Why the hell're you poking your damned nose in this?' Cody snarled. 'This little bitch don't mean diddly squat to you!'

'This ain't about the girl,' Drifter said grimly. 'It's about me and you three gutless, yellow-livered weasels!'

All three men flinched as if Drifter had slapped them.

'What the hell you waiting for?' Mace growled to Hudson. 'Kill him!'

'Be my pleathure,' Clay lisped. He faced Drifter, gloved hands hovering above his Colts. 'Fill your hand, dead man.'

21

Drifter smiled mirthlessly and prepared to draw. But before he could, footsteps came running up behind them and an authoritative voice barked: 'Hold it! All of you! Keep 'em leathered, *ja!*'

Drifter and the others turned and saw a squat, jowly man with a gray mustache and the face of a sad hound dog approaching. His name was Jan Van Dijk, though everyone called him 'Dutch', and pinned on his wolf-collared denim jacket was a deputy sheriff's badge. Stopping in front of the four men, he aimed a double-barreled shotgun at them and thumbed back both hammers, ending their quarrel.

'You men,' he said, his hard-edged voice tainted by a guttural Flemish accent, 'you no more make trouble, *ja?*'

Then, when no one backed down:

'I no tell you again!' he warned. 'You listen plenty to me, *ja?* Else I lock you in cage behind bars!'

Glad for an excuse to avoid a showdown with Drifter, Mace motioned to his brother. 'You heard the deputy, Cody. C'mon, let's head back to the ranch.'

The Iverson brothers started across the street.

Clay, about to follow them, could not resist turning to Drifter: 'You one lucky pilgrim, gunny. . . .'

'Took the words right out of my mouth – *shorty,*' Drifter taunted.

Clay flinched, stung by the insult. But unwilling to challenge the shotgun aimed at him by Deputy Dijk, he sneered at Drifter and lisped: 'Go ahead, gunny. Brag all you want. But juth remember thith: tomorrow ith another day. And from now on, no matter where you hide, I thall find you and gun you down!'

'You won't have to look far, *pendejo*,' Drifter promised. ' 'Cause I'll be hiding in plain sight!'

'All right, all right, no more you waste my time with these insults!' Deputy Dijk ordered. 'You two men, you do as I order, *ja*? Move!'

Grudgingly, Clay started after the Iverson brothers.

Deputy Dijk, satisfied that he'd diffused the situation, lowered the hammers of his shotgun and walked off toward the sheriff's office.

CHAPTER FOUR

Once the deputy had left, Drifter smiled reassuringly at Lydon, who'd been straightening her dress. 'Reckon you'll be fine now, missy.'

'Th-thank you,' she said, nervously chewing her lip. 'But what about you?'

'Me?'

'You shouldn't've butted in, mister.'

''Mean, I should've let them keep on mauling you?'

'N-no, but . . .' Lydon paused and chewed her lip again. 'You don't understand, mister. Th-those men, they work for Mr Stadtlander.'

'I know that, missy.'

'Then, how come you helped me?' she said, surprised. 'I mean, you must know how sore he'll be at you for butting in?'

Drifter smiled gently. 'You let me worry about Stillman J. Stadtlander, OK? This ain't the first time we've butted heads, and it surely won't be the last. Now, then,' he added, 'it's getting dark and I've ridden a far piece. . . .'

'I know.'

'You know?'

Lydon nodded. 'I was outside the livery stable when you were telling Mr Gustafson about your wore-out horse.'

''Mean, you were eavesdropping?'

'No, no, I wasn't. Honest! I was just, you know, walking past, on my way to meet my mother, and. . . .'

'Fair enough,' Drifter said, cutting her off. 'But, since you now know how bone-tired I am, let's go find your folks, so I can hit the hay. Where are they?'

'Momma's inside,' Lydon said, indicating the store, 'buying supplies.'

'And your pa?'

'He's home.'

Drifter frowned, surprised. 'Your pa, he let you and your mother come to town after sundown by yourselves?'

'He had no choice, mister. Yesterday, while he was plowing the south forty, he twisted his ankle. Today it's all black and blue, and so badly swollen he's having to hobble around on crutches. . . .' She broke off as a tall, vibrantly attractive woman with long, straw-colored hair and lively green eyes emerged from the store with a basket of groceries.

Drifter guessed she was in her early thirties, and though he couldn't pinpoint the exact reason, there was something about her that reminded him of the only woman he had ever loved: Helen Mercer. Helen had loved him with equal passion. But she'd also known that Drifter would never settle down. So she'd buried her love for him and remained married to her husband, Frank Mercer, an honest, hard-working farmer. Frank never suspected that Helen had betrayed him, and she never told him. But though she was never unfaithful again, the shame of betraying a decent honorable man haunted her from then on – especially when she found she was pregnant!

For Drifter, remembering Helen was like rubbing salt on a festering wound. Worse, it was a wound that could never be healed, because their one afternoon of illicit, passionate love-making had produced a child – a daughter, Emily, whom everyone naturally believed had been sired by Frank.

A wholesomely pretty child with an impish splash of freckles, she had golden brown eyes and long hair as yellow as lamplight. She possessed none of Frank's calm demeanor or patience, but was as wild and fiercely independent as her real father, Drifter. Also, like Drifter, she showed no interest in school or making friends, always preferring to be alone. And though bright and inquisitive, she set no goals for herself, and for years, while growing up, her future seemed bleak and uncertain. Then on turning sixteen, she inexplicably became interested in the law – specifically, the local sheriff and his duties. Every chance she got, she followed him around like a shadow. She also told everyone that despite being a woman, she intended to become a lawman – something that was almost unheard of at the time.

Helen and Frank, doubting she would ever reach her goal, tried to dissuade her. When they couldn't, they did what they thought was the best thing and enrolled her at St Marks, a convent in Las Cruces, New Mexico.

But Emily weathered the harsh discipline of the nuns, and while still a teenager, ran off to Oklahoma Territory. There, to hide her identity, she cut her hair boyishly short, changed her first name to Liberty out of respect for another deputy named Liberty, and taught herself to ride and shoot as well as any man.

Her dedication and abilities did not go unnoticed. Ada Carnutt, one of the first women ever to become a Deputy US Marshal, was so impressed by Liberty's fearlessness that she took her under her wing. And when Ada retired, she appointed Liberty as a temporary replacement until the US Marshal arrived. When he did, his 'old school' mentality was offended by a female deputy and he replaced her with a less quali-fied man. Angry and disappointed, Liberty returned to the fast-growing cattle town of Santa Rosa, hoping she could run for sheriff. But tragedy awaited her there, as she found that her folks had been murdered by marauding Comancheros. . . .

'Lydon!'

Drifter's thoughts of Liberty were interrupted by the lovely straw-haired woman. Vexed to see her daughter talking to a strange man, she angrily con-fronted them.

'What've I told you about talking to strangers?'

'Mother, he's not a – I mean, he is, but, well, he helped me, and . . .'

'*Helped* you?'

'Yes. These bad men who work for Mr Stadtlander kept on kissing me. . . .'

27

'*Kissing* you?'

'Yes, and, if this man hadn't chased them off, I don't know what would've happened.'

'I see. . . .'

'You should thank him, momma.'

'Y-yes, of course, I . . . uhm. . . .' Her mother paused, embarrassed, and offered her hand to Drifter. 'I'm Mrs Hannah Albright. Please forgive me for jumping to the wrong conclusion, Mr. . . ?'

'Folks call me Drifter, ma'am. And there's no need to apologize or fret yourself. In your place, I most likely would've throwed a shoe, too.' He smiled at Lydon, and said 'Glad I could be of help, missy,' and started to enter the store.

'Wait!' Hannah blocked his path and looked up at the tall gunfighter. 'I'm very grateful to you, Mr Drifter. And I know my husband, Drew, will be, too. What's more, I know he'd want to thank you personally.'

'That ain't necessary, ma'am.'

'Nevertheless,' Hannah continued, 'if you ever happen to be riding along the border just south of here and pass our ranch, the Bar-A, be sure to look in on us. I promise you, I'll fix you the best meal you've ever had!'

Drifter nodded his thanks. Then he winked playfully at Lydon, walked around Hannah and entered the haberdashery store.

CHAPTER FIVE

The store owner, Horace 'Mel' Melvin, prided himself on his inventory. 'If you can't find what you need,' he assured his customers, 'just let me know and I'll not only order it, but keep it in stock, so next time it'll be available.'

A large, balding, fleshy man who considered his big belly a sign of prosperity, he was at the cash register, ringing up a sale for a farmer, when he saw Drifter enter. He waved to show he'd be right with him. Drifter nodded in response and walked past the soda fountain to the rear of the store where there were shelves displaying men's and women's hats. He looked among the Stetsons for the same black, flat-crowned hat that his daughter had given him. There weren't any.

Disappointed, he started to walk away. Then, knowing he needed a hat to avoid getting sunstroke, he grudgingly turned back and tried to decide which other style he should buy. There was a wide selection, giving him plenty to choose from, and most men would have quickly found a suitable replacement. But

29

Drifter wasn't most men. He hated settling for anything other than exactly what he wanted – and now was no exception. He soon became frustrated, and was about to leave the store when he noticed a black felt hat that was like the hat he'd lost sitting atop a pile of discarded boxes in a dusty corner.

He went over and picked it up. It was far from new, and the wide brim and flat crown were badly scuffed. But when he tried it on, it fitted perfectly. Pleased, he was about to look around for a new canteen when Horace Melvin approached, his fat-bellied, hulking body blocking Drifter's path.

'Whoa, whoa, hold your horses,' he exclaimed, indicating the hat. 'You don't want to buy that ratty old thing.'

'Why not? It's what I want.'

'Maybe so. But I'm obliged to tell you something that will change your mind.'

Drifter gave him a doubtful look but said nothing.

'You see, my friend, this hat's not only second-hand. No, sir. That's the least of its problems. The ugly truth behind this hat is – well, it belonged to Bart Hagen.'

'So?'

Melvin smiled tolerantly, as if he were dealing with a guileless schoolboy, and said: 'Well, by your answer, you obviously never met the man.'

'No. But I've heard tell of him.'

'Did you also hear that he was the unluckiest fella who ever tied on spurs?'

'What's that got to do with his hat?'

'Plenty. Just ask Seth Perkins, our undertaker. He buried Hagen last week.'

'Yellow fever?'

'Try lead poisoning.'

Drifter frowned. 'That don't fit the Hagen I heard about. Everyone spoke kindly of him.'

'Everyone but Stadtlander's no-good, bullying rat of a son!'

'Slade?'

'The one and only. He and Hagen were playing poker at the Palace one night. Slade was losing bad, as usual, and accused Hagen of cheating. Hagen denied it and threw in his cards rather than get into a fight. But when he tried to leave, this no-good gunslinger that Stadtlander had recently hired – a trigger-happy little shootist named Clay Hudson – braced Hagen, forcing him to draw.'

'Hudson killed him?'

'Yep. Three slugs in the chest. Hagen was dead before he hit the floor. What's more, according to witnesses, Slade added insult to injury by insisting on searching Hagen. The other players protested, but were too scared of Hudson to interfere – and next thing you know, Slade pulled an ace out of Bart's sleeve. Of course, everyone knew Bart was no cheater and that Slade had somehow planted it there. But since they couldn't prove it, they didn't stop Slade from pocketing his losings as well as all of Bart's money, too.'

Drifter grunted disgustedly. 'Reckon the apple don't fall far from the tree, as they say. But that don't explain how you ended up with Hagen's hat.'

'Bart owed me for a new pair of rawhide boots. He was flat broke when he bought them. But I knew he was good for the money, on account he was working steady at the Eldorado Mine, so I carried him. Big mistake. Right after that, Bart was gunned down by Clay Hudson. His pals paid for his funeral. And Seth, after burying Hagen, gave me his hat, boots and saddle – you know, as compensation. I mean, sure, they were second-hand, but what the hell? I figured whatever I sold them for would help make up for part of the money Bart owed me.'

'Sounds fair,' Drifter said. 'So, how much are you asking for the hat?'

'You mean you still want it – even after knowing it was Bart's?'

'Why not? Lead poisoning ain't contagious.'

Melvin, lowering his voice as if sharing a confidence, said darkly: 'No, but folks around here, knowing how unlucky Hagen was, wouldn't buy anything he owned. And even if they would, I wouldn't sell it to them.'

'Why not?'

' 'Cause I wouldn't want whatever happened to them on my conscience.'

'*Conscience?*'

'Don't make it sound like I don't got one.'

'The thought never crossed my mind either way. So, then, who were you going sell his belongings to?'

'A stranger. Some fella just riding through. That way, if something bad happened to him, I wouldn't hear about it and feel responsible.'

Drifter grinned wolfishly. 'Don't worry, Mel. I won't hold you responsible if anything bad happens to me.'

'But. . . .'

32

'No "buts". I don't believe in luck, good or bad. Like it or not, sooner or later we all get what's coming to us. And wearing Bart Hagen's hat ain't going to alter that. So, name your price and I'll be on my way.'

Melvin shrugged. Money was the only language he understood, and indicating the cash register, he said: 'Suit yourself. C'mon, I'll ring it up for you.'

'Fair enough. First, though, I need shells and a new canteen. Mine's leaking.'

'Right there,' pointed Melvin. 'Last aisle over.'

A few minutes later Drifter emerged from the store. He was wearing the flat-crowned black hat and holding a new canteen, while a box of shells bulged in his pocket. It was still windy. And as he took a step forward, a sudden blustery gust threatened to blow away his hat. He grabbed for it and managed to grasp the brim.

It was lucky he did. Because just as Drifter reached for his hat, altering the angle of his head, a rifle shot rang out.

CHAPTER SIX

The bullet barely missed Drifter, who dived behind a
nearby water trough. There, he levered a round into
the chamber of his Winchester and cautiously peered
over the top.

Directly in front of him, riders and wagon-drivers
had reined up their horses, alarmed by the gunshot.
His gaze shifted. On both sides of the darkening,
wind-blown street people were cowering behind any
available cover. Drifter looked up and scanned the
rooftops and balconies of the buildings opposite but
saw no one threatening.

Puzzled, he was about to get up when he heard
horses galloping off. He looked toward the far end of
the street, and through the swirling dust caught a
glimpse of two horsemen riding out of town. Their
backs were to him, hiding their identity, but Drifter
recognized the horses and knew it was the Iverson
brothers. Promising himself that he'd take care of
them later, he rose and brushed himself off.

Slow, heavy footsteps plodded up behind him, and

someone said: 'Still dodging lead for a living, I see.'

Drifter turned and saw a huge man in his early fifties confronting him. A star glittered on his buckskin vest, while his beefy right hand rested on the butt of his holstered Colt .45. Yet, despite his imposing size, there was nothing threatening about him. Instead, he resembled a huge cuddly bear. He grinned amiably at Drifter, all the while chewing on a toothpick, and jokingly said: 'In case you don't know it, friend, dodging lead can be a mighty dangerous pastime.'

'Maybe if you'd do your job,' Drifter needled, 'I wouldn't need to dodge – lead or anything else.'

'I'll keep that in mind,' Sheriff Lonnie Forbes said. He rolled the toothpick between his tobacco-stained lips to the other side of his mouth and held out a big, thick-fingered hand to Drifter. 'Meanwhile, no hard feelings, I hope?'

Drifter had no respect for the sheriff and was tempted to ignore his outstretched hand. But deciding that he had nothing to gain by deliberately provoking the big lawman, he grudgingly shook hands. 'Nary a one, Lonnie.'

'Fine, fine. Nothing I hate worse than misunderstandings.'

'So you keep telling everybody.'

'Yeah. Reckon I do. But it's true. Way I figure, misunderstandings ain't only annoying, but they can prove to be mighty perilous for a fella's health.' Sheriff Forbes paused, scratched his head, and again rolled the toothpick between his lips before adding: 'Come to think of it, it's been a spell since I last seen you around.'

Drifter gave a shrug that could have meant any-thing.

'What brings you to my neck of the woods, anyhow?'

'Just drifting.'

'Uh-huh . . .' Sheriff Forbes considered Drifter's reply, then absently picked his nose before saying: 'Well, as the Good Lord knows, I ain't one to doubt another man's word. But, to be perfectly honest, I find your answer tough to swallow.'

'How so?'

'Well, if drifting's your only reason for being here, that means no one was expecting you.'

'So?'

'So, I got to ask myself, how come someone just tried to kill you?'

Drifter shrugged noncommittally.

'Unless, of course, trouble followed you here?'

Again, Drifter just shrugged.

The sheriff pinned him with a cold, hard-eyed look. 'You wouldn't be trying to rile me, now, would you?'

'Not intentionally.'

'Then, damn it, tell me what the hell that shooting was about?'

'You're asking the wrong person.'

'Then who should I be asking?'

'The Iverson brothers.'

'Oh, don't worry, I intend to get around to them,' Sheriff Forbes said. 'But right now, friend, I'm asking you. And I'd be mighty obliged if you'd quit playing me like a broken violin and give me a straight answer.'

Drifter grinned wolfishly. 'Maybe they didn't like

my new hat.'

'Your hat?' Sheriff Forbes frowned and looked at Drifter's hat as if seeing it for the first time. Momentarily, he couldn't place where he'd seen it before. Then it dawned on him, and he exclaimed: 'Wait a minute! Ain't that Bart . . .?'

'Hagen's hat, yeah.'

'Then how come you're wearing it?'

'I needed a hat. It was for sale. I bought it. End of trail. Now, if there's nothing else, sheriff . . .' Drifter started to leave.

'Whoa! Hang on!'

Drifter paused and faced the big lawman.

'Before you go, friend, I got one last question for you: I ain't seen your two sidekicks around lately. Have you?'

'Not recently.'

'How recently is not recently?'

Drifter shrugged. 'Last time I saw Latigo Rawlins was . . . maybe six or seven months ago.'

'Where?'

'Waco.'

'Waco?' Sheriff Forbes briefly searched his memory and then it hit him. 'Of course!' he exclaimed. 'Damn it, where's my dumb brains? I should've known.'

'Known what?'

'That it was you and Latigo who busted Gabe Moonlight out of jail before the law could stretch his neck for gunning down them two drunken cowboys.'

'They weren't cowboys,' Drifter said bitterly. 'They were low-life, scum-sucking bounty hunters!'

'Figures. . . .' Sheriff Forbes absently picked his

37

nose again. 'What happened? Did they find out that Gabe and the outlaw, Mesquite Jennings, were one and the same *hombre*, and tried to collect the reward?'

'Close.'

'And now they're chewing daisies?'

'Seemed fair.'

Sheriff Forbes briefly considered Drifter's answer, then spat out the toothpick, took a fresh one from his vest pocket and stuck it between his lips. 'We-e-ll,' he drawled, 'I can't say I'm sorry for their loss. I've always liked Gabe, hot temper and all, so I'm glad they didn't kill him.'

'He'll be thrilled to hear that.'

Sheriff Forbes ignored Drifter's sarcasm and said enviously: 'So will two fine-looking whores I know. To hear them talk, whoring's a bust without Gabe around.'

'That's 'cause he's never learned to keep it in his pants.'

'From what I've heard, he's never had to.'

'True,' Drifter agreed, adding: 'We all done talking?'

'Sure. But first, here's a piece of free advice: if you're just drifting through, like you say, then you're welcome here. But if you're figuring on gunning down Slade Stadtlander, then I'd be obliged if you'd ride on.'

'Come sun-up, I intend to. But right now, I got me a powerful thirst to quench. So, I'll say *vaya con dios* and be on my way.' With a casual throwaway salute, Drifter continued along the boardwalk in the direction of the Copper Palace.

Sheriff Forbes watched him, mind churning suspiciously. Then deciding to keep tabs on the prickly gunman, he muttered, 'Reckon I'll join you,' and ambled after Drifter.

CHAPTER SEVEN

The Copper Palace was even more crowded than usual, forcing late comers to spill out on to the boardwalk fronting the notorious old saloon. Tough, rowdy cowboys, grubby-bearded miners and slick-talking traveling salesmen – no matter who they were, they all had something in common: they were raucously drunk and planned on getting even drunker. Encouraging them were several rouge-painted whores in bright gaudy dresses laced up so tight their powdered breasts bulged out invitingly.

Whores were cheap and plentiful in Santa Rosa, as well as all the other cattle towns along the borders of New Mexico and Arizona. This meant competition among them was so fierce, they were willing to do anything short of murder in order to please their pimps. This included accepting money from the various saloon owners, who paid them on the condition that the whores lure in customers, and then, once they were inside, coax them into buying cheap, watered-down whiskey at the bar before dragging them upstairs for sex in their rooms.

Drifter, aware of the whores' tactics, paused on the boardwalk near the saloon and scanned the faces of the boisterous men and women gathered out front. He recognized most of them from other border towns and mining camps and felt safe among them. As for the strangers, despite not knowing them, he decided they did not appear to be gunmen ready to bushwhack him for past grievances, but seemed only interested in kissing and fondling the whores.

Satisfied, Drifter squeezed through the crowd and pushed on through the batwing doors into the saloon. Once inside, he stood with his back to the wall and surveyed the mass of seedy, unruly humanity separating him from the bar.

Most of the men were happily drunk and not looking for trouble; but in one corner a sober, belligerent miner was arguing with two drunken cowboys who were trying to drag his whore away. Their foul cursing was so loud, it almost drowned out the honky-tonk music being played by a fat old piano player in a yellow-and-green plaid suit and a natty bowler hat, who sat pounding a battered upright.

Drifter pushed his way through the jostling mob to the bar. On his way he passed the poker tables facing the stairs leading up to the second floor. Several big, floppy-breasted whores were seductively trying to coax the players to quit playing cards and join them upstairs. Two of the whores recognized Drifter as he passed. They smiled, but knew him well enough not to try to entice him up to their rooms.

On reaching the long, crowded bar, Drifter elbowed aside a bleary-eyed, half-drunk salesman and took his place at the far end. The two mustachioed, white-aproned bartenders were busy serving drinks; but one, a grizzled veteran named Harry O', on recognizing Drifter, took a moment to pour him a beer and a shot of whiskey and set them on the bar before him.

Drifter nodded his thanks and paid for the boilermaker with a silver dollar. He then took a gulp of beer and chased it down with the whiskey. The drink didn't fully quench his thirst, but nectar couldn't have tasted better. Drifter belched, and after another satisfying gulp, leaned against the bar and tried to forget how tired he was, and just to relax and enjoy the moment.

He'd almost accomplished his goal when he felt something round and hard jab him in the back. He knew instantly it was a gun barrel. He stiffened and slowly raised his hands, glanced over his shoulder – and saw Clay Hudson smirking at him.

'Juth turn around, gunny,' the little gunman lisped. 'And keep your hanth up.'

Grudgingly, Drifter obeyed him.

'Now, with your left hand, pleath take out your iron and thet it on the bar.'

Drifter hesitated, tempted to take a chance and draw. But sensing he couldn't clear leather before Clay shot him, he lowered his left hand down across his chest toward his holstered gun.

Behind him, the men drinking at the bar hastily backed up, out of the line of fire, while everyone else in the saloon grew deathly quiet.

Drifter's left hand now reached the butt of his pistol. But before he could pull the weapon from its holster, Sheriff Forbes suddenly stepped out of the crowd behind Clay and pistol-whipped him across the head.

Clay crumpled without a sound, his gun dropping to the sawdust-covered floor.

Everyone gasped and sagged with relief.

'I like your timing,' Drifter wryly told the sheriff.

'Enough to buy me a drink?'

'How about a whole bottle?'

Sheriff Forbes chuckled. 'Thanks. But you know how some folks are. They'd most likely get the wrong impression, and figure you was trying to corrupt . . .' he broke off as his deputy pushed out of the crowd and joined him.

'You be OK, *ja?*' Van Dijk asked anxiously.

Sheriff Forbes nodded and thumbed at Clay. 'Lock this trash up, Dutch.'

'Sure, sure, I do for you right away.' Deputy Dijk knelt beside Clay, handcuffed his hands behind his back and dragged the now conscious but still dazed gunman to his feet. 'You! Get up! Come with me, *ja?*' He pushed Clay ahead of him, the crowd of onlookers separating to allow both men through.

'Now,' Sheriff Forbes said, grinning at Drifter. 'About that drink, friend. . . ?'

CHAPTER EIGHT

Later that same night an exhausted Drifter, at Lars' urging, slept in the loft of the livery stable. Normally a restless sleeper who awoke several times during the night, tonight was different: he fell asleep almost as soon as he crawled under his blanket, and didn't awaken until the next morning, when the shrill crowing of a nearby rooster penetrated his brain.

Groggy, Drifter raised himself up on his elbows, yawning and stretching. In front of him, through the open loft doorway, he noticed dawn was approaching. It was a glorious sight. The slowly rising sun had tinted the clouds, turning them pink, yellow and mauve as they drifted over the pale, waning moon.

Drifter, grateful for the much-needed sleep, lay back, arms folded behind his head, his senses enjoying the aroma of the sweet-smelling hay piled about him. .. . .

He might have drifted off again, but other roosters began to greet the morning in unison. Their incessant crowing erased any thought of sleep from Drifter's mind. Rising, he fought off the shivers, pulled on his jeans, descended the ladder and washed his face in the bucket of water Lars had left him at the rear of the stable. He then forked some hay into the stall holding his sorrel, climbed back up the ladder and finished dressing.

Restless and uneasy about staying too long in one place, he saddled up and rode out of town. A few early-bird storekeepers waved as Drifter passed. He nodded to show he'd seen them. Then, tempted by the smell of bacon and waffles coming from the Blue Hat Café, he considered stopping to eat. But then he remembered he still had leftovers from his last meal in his saddlebag, and ever frugal, decided to fix his own breakfast.

Once out of town, he reined up beside a spring that bubbled up from the sand by a rocky outcrop. Early daylight allowed him to see anyone approaching from all directions. Feeling safe, Drifter dismounted and left the sorrel contentedly drinking while he built a fire out of dried brush. Fanning the glowing coals with his hat until flames broke out, he hunkered down, set his frying pan on the fire and cooked up a chunk of sizzling bacon and the last of the egg yolks he kept in a small tin flask.

While waiting for the food to finish cooking, he poured himself a mug of coffee from the old blackened kettle boiling on the embers. The coffee was so bitter, he wanted to spit it out. But it was all he had, so he grimaced it down, then settled back to enjoy his bacon and eggs out of the pan.

While he ate, a coyote yip-yipped in the distance. Usually, the mournful howling increased Drifter's feeling of loneliness. But today was different. For some reason that escaped him, he found the howling comforting, as if he and the coyote were companions sharing a mutual loneliness, and he allowed himself a quick smile.

After he'd finished eating, Drifter washed his utensils at the spring and dried them on his shirt-tail before returning them to his saddlebag. He then sat down, took out the makings, rolled and lit a smoke and leaned back against the rocks, hoping to enjoy a few rare moments of peaceful pleasure.

It wasn't to be.

Lately, for some unknown reason, he'd become too troubled by his violent past to fully relax. Eyes open or closed, it didn't matter. There was no escape. His mind was haunted by the faces of the belligerent fame-seeking gunmen he'd been forced to kill. Yet it hadn't always been that way. As a younger man, he'd been able to shoot someone, shrug it off and then later drown the memory with a few shots of tequila. But now, as he closed in on fifty, it was becoming more and more difficult, and Drifter wondered why that was. . . .

CHAPTER NINE

By mid-morning, the colorful dawn had been replaced by a bright blue sky sprinkled with fluffy white clouds that lessened the intense heat whenever they passed over the sun. Drifter, having spent his entire life in the blazing desert heat, had taught himself to ignore the weather and to function normally no matter what the conditions were.

Today was no exception. As he rode slowly toward the border, alongside the miles of white fencing that marked the southern boundary of the Albright ranch, he had only two things on his mind: to enjoy a bottle of tequila at the nearest cantina and perhaps pleasure himself with a willing, pretty *señorita*.

The thought of tequila made Drifter lick his parched lips. Thankfully, he didn't have far to go. Being familiar with all the little pueblos scattered along the US-Mexican border, he knew the closest one was San Pablo – a collection of old, dilapidated sun-baked hovels no more than two hours' ride ahead.

Eager to enjoy himself as soon as possible, Drifter kneed the sorrel into an easy canter that effortlessly ate up the miles. As he loped along, he noticed a cattle-gate in the fencing a short distance ahead. The gusting winds that continually swept the endless canyons and deserts had blown the gate open, as if inviting him in. It made him remember Hannah's offer of a fine home-cooked meal and he was tempted to ride through the gate and follow the trail to the Albright homestead, the cabin and barn of which he could see among the foothills. But then his conscience kicked in, reminding him about how he and Hannah felt about each other, and deciding not to cause turmoil in another man's marriage, Drifter grudgingly rode on.

But there was no dodging destiny. He'd only ridden another mile or so, when he saw a rider galloping toward him from the homestead. He couldn't tell who it was, but by urgent the way they were waving he guessed they were anxious to catch up to him. Wary but also curious, Drifter reined up, hand on his hol-stered Dragoon Colt pistol and watched as the rider drew closer and closer . . . until finally he could see their face and realized it was Lydon.

The sight of her reminded Drifter of his daughter, Emily, and momentarily he felt a stab of remorse. But before he could punish himself further by dwelling on the years of painful memories and separation, he was saved by Lydon. Reining up before him, she blurted out how she'd seen him while swinging on her corral gate.

'Good thing I did, too,' she scolded. 'Because you, you meanie, weren't going to stop, were you? You was going to ride on by without even a hoot or a hidee!'

Drifter shrugged. 'Truth be told, missy, I hadn't decided yet.'

'Then I'll decide for you, Mr-Quint-Longley! 'Cause if I don't, I might never see you again. Besides, Pa Drew wants to meet you. Mother told him about how you scared off the Iversons, and he wants to thank you personally.'

Gratitude, like praise, always made Drifter feel uncomfortable and inwardly he grimaced. Also, he didn't want to tempt himself by being around Hannah.

'I'm sorry, missy, but. . . .'

Lydon cut him off. 'Please, mister,' she begged. 'Do it for me, huh?'

'You?'

'Yeah. If you don't show up, momma will find a way to blame me for it and give me a spanking. Besides,' she added, indicating the cabin, 'it ain't like I'm asking you to ride miles out of your way, is it?'

Drifter, irked that he'd painted himself into a corner, grudgingly said: 'OK. I'll agree on one condition, missy. You ride ahead and tell your folks I'm coming.'

Lydon beamed. 'Yay! Just watch my dust!' Joyfully, she kicked up her pony and galloped back to the cabin.

'Happy now?' Drifter growled, admonishing himself. 'I mean, you just stepped in a whole puddle of trouble. . . .'

CHAPTER TEN

Later, when Drifter rode into the Albright front yard, he was confronted by a large gray-and-white gander that flapped its wings and honked challengingly at him. The commotion served as an alarm, and within moments, two wolf-dog mongrels charged up, barking and nipping at the sorrel's heels. Drifter yelled at them and threatened them with his coiled lasso. Intimidated, they slunk away and stood growling at him from under a rusting buckboard.

Drifter looked around but could see no sign of Lydon. But as he reined up before the sturdily built log cabin, the door opened and out stepped her mother, Hannah. She shooed away the gander and the barking mongrels and smiled up at Drifter.

'Please, pay them no mind,' she apologized. 'They're really not mean or vicious. It's just that, well, we get so few visitors way out here, they don't know how to treat them.'

'Understandable, ma'am. . . .' Drifter tried not to look at Hannah, fearing she'd sense how he felt toward her. But he found her so damned beautiful, he couldn't take his eyes off her. Equally captivating was the fact that she'd made no effort to make herself more attractive as most woman he knew did before greeting a man, but had merely pulled her long straw-colored hair back in a pleasingly simple bun. He also noticed that her lovely tanned face was free of rouge and lipstick, and her plain homespun dress was faded from constant washing. It was also patched at both elbows, while its color matched her wide-set, warm green eyes. To some men she might have been nothing more than an attractive frontier woman. But to Drifter, just the sight of her made his heart leap in the same way it had once leaped whenever he saw Helen Mercer.

Hannah's voice interrupted Drifter's thoughts, jolting him back to the present, so that he caught her last words: '. . . what a lovely surprise!'

'It's kind of you to say so, ma'am. But the truth is, I didn't plan on intruding. It's just that, well, it was mighty hard to say "no" to your daughter.'

Hannah laughed, a spontaneous little laugh that was as pleasingly honest as creek water splashing over rocks.

'Yes, I'm sure it was,' she said, amused by the thought of her pushy daughter. 'Lydon can be most, how shall I say, *persuasive* when she sets her mind to it. As for intruding, Mr Drifter, never worry yourself about that. Our whole family owes you a debt that we'll never be able to fully repay.'

Drifter sensed that Hannah was speaking from her heart, and couldn't find words to respond. There followed an embarrassing moment of silence.

Hannah broke it first. 'Please, forgive my bad manners, Mr Drifter. Won't you step down and join me – *us* – for lunch? Earlier, when I was at the window, I saw you coming and sent Lydon to fetch her father. They should be back shortly, but these days, unfortunately – well, I don't know if my daughter told you, but Drew has been hobbled by an ankle injury and is finding it difficult to handle even the simplest of chores.'

'Yeah, she did mention how he'd twisted it.'

'Quite badly, I'm afraid,' Hannah said, adding: 'Then you will break bread with us, Mr Drifter?'

'On one condition.'

'What's that?'

'You quit calling me mister.'

'What should I call you then?'

'Just plain Drifter will do fine.'

'Very well. Drifter it is. Unless of course . . .'

'Go on.'

'. . . you have a Christian name. Then, frankly, I'd prefer to call you by that.'

Drifter hesitated, reluctant to give out his name since it reminded him of his years in the orphanage. But then he surprised himself by saying: 'It's Quint, ma'am. Quint Longley.'

Hannah silently repeated his name to herself and then smiled. 'That's a fine name indeed. Has strength to it. And dignity. So if you don't mind, from now on I'll call you Quint. Oh, and please, call me Hannah, not ma'am. As you'll soon find out, there's little time for formalities way out here. . . .'

She broke off as she smelled something burning,

and then exclaimed: 'Oh, my goodness! You'll have to excuse me, Mr Drift – I mean, Quint. But I've got to take the stew off the stove before it's ruined. Oh, and by the way,' she added as Drifter dismounted, 'feel free to water your horse and wash up, if you're so inclined. The pump's over there.' She pointed at a hand pump at one end of a water trough facing the barn, and before Drifter could respond, hurried indoors.

CHAPTER ELEVEN

Inside, the single-level log cabin was larger and more comfortable than Drifter had expected. Besides two bedrooms, there was also a small kitchen with a stone sink, a pot-bellied stove, and a living area filled with rough-hewn wooden furniture, some of which faced a rock fireplace with a hearth. Presently there was no fire, but Drifter guessed that during winter a pile of burning logs would keep the snowbound cabin warm and cozy. As for light, a single window facing east let in enough sunlight so that the hand-hammered copper candelabra hanging over the table was presently not needed.

That same sunlight showed an oil painting of a young Hannah hanging on the wall above the fireplace. In it, she wore a beautiful white Victorian wedding dress. A delicate lacy veil covered her head and face, while in her lap her white-gloved hands held a bouquet of red roses. She looked demure and innocent, yet at the same time the artist had cleverly captured an inner mischievousness behind her bewitching smile.

As Drifter stood admiring the painting, he felt a tug at his side. He looked down and saw it was Lydon. She had on a dress and shoes and smelled of the same lye soap that he'd used earlier when he'd washed up.

'Momma's mighty pretty, ain't she?' she said proudly.

Drifter nodded.

'Everybody says so. But guess what?'

'What?'

'I know a secret that nobody else knows.'

'About your mother?'

'Uh-huh. Want to hear it?'

'If it's a secret, missy, then maybe you shouldn't tell me.'

'No, no, it's OK. Momma won't mind. She says you're like one of the family. Which should make you feel mighty proud,' Lydon added, ' 'cause I've never heard her say that about nobody else before. Not never.'

Drifter, surprised and embarrassed by the compliment, remained stoically silent.

Eager to reveal her secret, Lydon pointed at the painting. 'See that dress and veil momma's wearing?'

'Uh-huh.'

'Her mother and grandmother wore them back when they got wed.'

'Nothing wrong with hand-me-downs.'

'Wasn't just her dress and veil, neither. It was her gloves and her shoes, too. See, when she married Pa Drew, they was both dirt poor and couldn't afford to buy no fancy wedding clothes.'

'No shame in that.'

'Maybe not. But Mother told me she felt awful bad, on account it was her fault they didn't have no money.'

'How do you mean?'

'Well . . . you see, her daddy was rich. Plenty rich. And his family was what big city folks call, um, "well bred". And 'cause of that, he didn't want her to marry a poor dirt farmer like Pa Drew. But Momma loved him so much, she didn't care and married him anyway. And 'cause she did, her father got powerful angry. So angry in fact, he had his lawyers change his will, so that legally Mother was no longer part of the family.'

' 'Mean . . . he disinherited her?'

'Yeah, yeah, that's the word she used: dis-in-inherit-whatever. . . .' Lydon broke off as she saw Drew approaching on homemade crutches.

'OK, you two,' he said affably. 'Come to the table, please. Food's ready.'

'You can sit next to me,' Lydon told Drifter. 'Can't he, Pa Drew?'

'Why sure. That'd be just fine.' He slipped Drifter an amused wink, whispered, 'I think you've stolen her heart,' and moved away before Drifter could respond.

The remark caught Drifter off guard. He just stood there, imposingly tall and remote, trying to decide if he should allow himself to be pleased by Lydon's affection, or if he should brush it off as a dangerous weakness – a weakness that had to be kept plugged up, like the chinks between a cabin's log walls, or eventually it would destroy his ability to endure a life of endless, lonely drifting.

'C'mon,' Lydon said, grabbing his hand and

leading him to the rough-hewn wooden table. 'Sit here, next to me.'

Drifter obeyed. And despite his reluctance to lower his guard and become part of a loving family, he couldn't deny that their warmth made him feel good.

Hannah now came to the table and served them each a hunk of home-baked bread and a bowl of hearty meat stew that earlier Drifter had seen cooking in a cauldron on the stove.

It was a moment of pure domesticity. And in that moment, Drifter looked at Hannah and tried to picture himself as a diligent, hard-working, honest farmer responsible not only for feeding his wife and daughter but for making sure they were safe from outlaws and renegade Comanches; while at the same time obligated to plow the hundred-odd acres of flat, sun-parched grassland he had bought with his savings before asking Hannah's now-deceased father for her hand. It had been merely a symbolic gesture on Drew's part because he was certain that he'd be turned down. But he was honorable enough to believe that he owed it to Hannah out of respect for both her and their marital vows.

His integrity didn't go unrewarded. Grateful, Hannah showed her appreciation by bluntly warning her father that if he didn't give Drew his permission, willingly or unwillingly, she'd shame him and the family even further by eloping.

Drifter, unable to picture himself handling that sort of pressure, shifted his gaze from Hannah and studied the man seated across the table from him.

Although Drew Albright wasn't much to look at,

Drifter had to admit there was something instantly likable about him. A stocky man much shorter than Drifter, he had receding brown hair and a long thin nose that had been broken when he was thrown from a wild mustang that he was trying to break. His best feature, though, Drifter decided, were his clear blue eyes. They were bright with honesty, and would have been appealing if they hadn't been so close together and somewhat sunken. To make matters worse, his narrow, pinched, thin-lipped mouth hid his cheerful personality and made him look perpetually grim.

But Drifter had lived long enough to know that looks alone didn't make a man. From stories he'd heard while drifting throughout the territory, folks both admired and respected Drew for his honesty and lack of conceit, pointing out that he was quick to admit that he couldn't understand why a woman as beautiful, desirable and smart as Hannah had ever married him, especially since it was against her father's wishes and came at such a personal price.

'All right everybody, time to eat!' Hannah's cheery voice interrupted Drifter's thoughts. He watched as she finished serving the food, then sat beside her husband and asked him to say grace.

Drew nodded agreeably. Clasping his hands together, he waited for Hannah and Lydon to do the same, lowered his head and closed his eyes in prayer.

Drifter, unable to remember when he'd last said grace, felt obliged to join in.

When Drew was done asking the Lord to bless their food, and thanking Him for His love and treasured gift of life, he whispered 'Amen', and unclasped his hands. He then looked up and smiled at Drifter, adding: 'I'm glad you could join us for this humble meal. As I'm sure Hannah has told you: living way out here, we seldom have the pleasure of guests.'

Drifter grinned wryly. 'I don't know nothing about guests being a pleasure, *compadre.* Frankly, most folks I've come across, I could gladly do without. But I do know this: I'd never call this food humble. In fact, it looks to be about the best meal I've had since – well, since I can't remember when.'

Lydon giggled. 'Bet you're just saying that to be polite.'

'That's enough, child,' Hannah said sharply. 'One more word out of you and you won't be able to sit down for a week!'

'Your mother's right,' Drew scolded. 'Shame on you, young lady. Where are your manners? You know you're not allowed to speak at the table.'

Lydon rolled her eyes and muttered something inaudible under her breath.

'What did you say?' Hannah demanded.

'Nothing.'

'Don't make it worse by lying. Please answer my question.'

Lydon made a face. 'How can I answer, momma, if I ain't allowed to talk at the table?'

'Now you're just being plain silly! You know the rules. You may speak when spoken to. Now, for the last time, child, tell me what you said.'

Peeved, Lydon chewed her lip before saying: 'Well, if you must know, I said, if it wasn't for me, you wouldn't have no guest. Ain't that so?' she added to Drifter.

He hesitated, then sheepishly admitted to Hannah and Drew: 'In your daughter's defense, she did have a lot to do with why I'm here.'

'See, mother,' Lydon said smugly. 'Just because you don't believe me, don't mean I ain't telling the truth.'

Hannah wearily shook her head and half jokingly said to Drifter: 'You know, Quint, more and more I'm beginning to appreciate why you keep drifting.'

CHAPTER TWELVE

After they'd eaten, Drifter and Drew left Lydon helping her mother wash the dishes and went out for a smoke. But the weather was against them. During lunch storm clouds had gathered overhead and the two men were no sooner comfortably seated on a hay bale when lightning flashed. Rumbling thunder followed. Drew stopped packing tobacco into the bowl of his clay pipe and glared up at the dark, threatening sky.

'Ain't it always the way?' he grumbled. 'I swear, Quint, 'tween work, chores and bad weather a man's barely got time to enjoy his pipe. . . .' Thunder boomed again, closer now, hiding his words. And even as the two men looked skyward, more lightning crackled. This time it was forked, a series of menacing zig-zagging flashes that pierced the ominous black clouds like flaming daggers and stabbed the surrounding desert landscape.

'We'd better fill those with water,' Drew said, indicating two wooden buckets beside the water trough. 'You know, just in case lightning strikes the cabin or

61

the barn and maybe sets one of the roofs on fire!'

Drifter nodded and handed Drew his crutches. But they needn't have worried. Even as they went to the water trough, Nature decided to end the potential danger and it abruptly started to rain.

Drenched by the sudden downpour, the two men ducked, cursing, into the barn. There, as they wiped themselves dry, the thunder and lightning continued outside.

'That settles it,' Drew said. 'You're staying here tonight, Quint. No argument,' he added as Drifter started to protest. 'You're staying, and that's it!'

'Fair enough,' said Drifter, relenting. 'Just so long as your wife don't object.'

'Object'?' Drew chuckled wryly. 'Just the opposite, my friend. Why, Hannah would have my head if I didn't insist you stayed. Fact is,' he added, 'you'd make both of us mighty happy if you stayed on for more than tonight.'

'On account of your ankle, you mean?'

'Right. Speaking of which, I'd be lying if I didn't say I could sorely use your help right now. There's fields to be plowed, crops that need harvesting, grain to be stored, and if that ain't enough, the cabin walls need re-mudding before the winter snows come!'

'Well, I'd like to help you,' Drifter said, still worried that he might not be able to restrain his feelings for Hannah. 'But I ain't sure how much use I'd be.'

'How do you mean?'

'Well . . .' Drifter began, and then paused as he searched for a lie to conceal the truth. 'I've worked a heap of different jobs in my life – cowboying, wrangling, line camps, even for the railroad for a spell – but farming and repairing cabin walls? Hell's fire, *compadre*, that's a bronc of a different color.'

'I know that,' Drew said. 'And I won't be offended if you turn me down. But will you at least think about it? Overnight, say? And let me know come sun-up?'

'Fair enough,' Drifter said. 'Sun-up it is.'

That night it continued to pour. Drifter could hear the rain pounding on the barn roof as he lay under his blanket in the hayloft. He was unable to sleep. All he could think about was Hannah. As hour after restless hour passed, troubling questions kept cropping up. One especially haunted him: would he be able to keep away from her if he stayed and helped Drew? Or, as he feared, would their constant daily contact slowly erode his resistance until lust eventually destroyed his integrity and drove him to do something he'd always regret?

Of course, he reflected as the thought hit him, he was assuming that Hannah had the same feelings for him. Which, when he thought about it, was a mite egotistical on his part. After all, why would a woman who'd married young, a woman who had probably never known another man before Drew, be drawn to him? Or, even more illogical, why would she suddenly throw caution to the winds and sneak off for an afternoon of illicit love-making?

Truth was, she most likely wouldn't.

But then Drifter remembered the look in Hannah's eyes whenever she looked at him . . . and it made him nervous. As a result, he promised himself that no matter the circumstances, he'd never let it happen.

Still, deep inside him, where the truth cannot be ignored, he couldn't quiet his nagging conscience. It kept reminding him of the fiery minister at the orphanage, who treated the youngsters like hardened sinners, constantly preaching to them about how their sinful lust for sex would lead them into the awaiting arms of the Devil. This was because, despite all their futile effort to control their Satanic urges, they would fail, for although the spirit might be willing, the flesh was weak.

The ancient sermon drummed in Drifter's ears. It made him wonder if, despite their resolve, there might come a moment when he or Hannah would succumb to the ever-present temptation. . . .

Unwilling to take that chance, Drifter finally decided to turn Drew down and to ride on. Once he'd made that decision, he felt better about himself. And as the crowing roosters announced the arrival of dawn, he crawled out of his blanket and sleepily pulled on his jeans and boots. Then grabbing his towel and soap, he descended the ladder that was propped against the floor of the hayloft and pushed open the barn door. Outside, the rainstorm had finally passed. But it was bitterly cold and damp, and a dense mist greeted Drifter as he stepped out of the barn. Shivering, he hurried to the water trough. A thin layer of ice covered the water and for a moment he was tempted to return to his warm blanket and wait until sun-up before washing.

It was then he heard footsteps approaching behind him. He turned, expecting to see Drew. But it was

Hannah, looking ghostly luminous in the misty dawn light. She wore a gray woolen shawl around her shoulders, had an apron tied about her slim waist and her long, straw-colored hair hung loosely about her lovely face. From a few steps away, she appeared to be in control of her emotions. But as she came closer, Drifter saw how red and puffy her eyes were and how exhausted she looked, and he knew that she hadn't gotten any sleep either.

Stopping before him, she said almost accusingly: 'You're leaving, aren't you?'

'Yep.'

'Because of me, right?'

'Because of us,' he corrected.

'No, no, you mustn't blame yourself for . . .'

He raised his hand, stopping her, and said: 'Please, ma'am, don't deny it. I saw it in your eyes every time you looked at me.'

Hannah reddened. 'It was that obvious? Shame on me.'

'Shame on us both.'

Embarrassed, Hannah sighed and looked away. 'You know, Quint,' she said, as if trying to justify herself, 'I'm not a woman of easy virtue.'

'Never figured you were.'

'I'm also happily married, but. . . .'

He waited, tight-lipped and silent, for her to continue.

' . . . the truth is, I'm also lonely. Drew is a fine, honorable man and no woman could ask for a more loving husband . . . or a better father for her child. . . .'

65

'But?'

'He's always so preoccupied by the land and every-thing he needs to do with it that, well, sometimes I feel unwanted ... or needed ... invisible even ... someone who only exists when my husband thinks it's time to acknowledge me. . . .'

Drifter wished he could find the words to comfort her. But as usual, for him, silence was his only companion.

Hannah now looked up at him, saying: 'Would it do any good if I asked you to stay? Not for me or for us,' she added quickly, 'but for Drew's sake?'

'Hell, it's for Drew's sake that I'm riding on.'

'Even though he – all of us – desperately need you to stay?'

'Yeah, but at what price?'

'The farm – our future.'

'Our?'

'Drew's, mine and Lydon's.'

'Sorry, I don't get your drift. I mean, how does my staying on fit in with that?'

'It's simple. If we lose the farm, God only knows where we will end up. We don't have any savings, so most likely it'd be the poor house. But if we can hang on to the farm, we'd at least have a roof over our heads *and* a possible future. Oh, I know trying to eke out a living here will be hard,' Hannah continued, as if warning herself, 'dreadfully hard. But I also know that if Drew and I set our minds to it, we can – no, we *will* make it work!'

'Sounds a mite like wishful thinking to me.'

'Only time will tell.'

Drifter looked long and hard at Hannah. On top of desiring her, he greatly admired her determination. He was also man enough to hope she was right. But, ever the realist, he still couldn't convince himself that everything would work out between her and Drew – not so long as she also loved him.

'I promise you this,' she said, as if reading his mind, 'much as I want you – and God only knows how *much* I want you – if you'll stay and help Drew out, I'll do everything in my power to remain faithful to my husband. You have my solemn word on that, Quint.'

Drifter, unable to find anything suitable to add, remained tight-lipped and silent.

Hannah didn't seem to notice. 'Well,' she added, as if relieved, 'I've spoken my piece, Mr Longley. Now it's entirely up to you.' She turned and started back to the cabin. But on reaching the door, she paused and looked back at him. 'Breakfast will be ready shortly.'

Drifter nodded but didn't answer.

'Regardless of your decision, Quint, please join us. Both Lydon and my husband will be awfully disappointed if you ride on without so much as a goodbye.'

'Don't worry, Hannah. I'll be there.'

'Good. And make sure you bring your appetite.' Giving him a quick smile, she entered the cabin and closed the door behind her.

Drifter stared after her, heart thudding, mind churning, guts drained. . . .

CHAPTER THIRTEEN

Drifter said little during breakfast. But in his mind, a battle raged as he again tried to choose between obeying his conscience and riding on, or allowing himself to be persuaded by Hannah's urging to stay and help Drew. It was no easy decision, and for most of the meal, Drifter couldn't decide what to do.

Fortunately, it was not yet sun-up, so there was still time before he had to give Drew his answer. And to Drew's credit, he didn't try to pressure Drifter into a decision. Instead, while the four of them wolfed down eggs and bacon and flakey, hot buttered biscuits, he kept his conversation centered on his family, alternating between gently chiding Lydon for not doing her homework or her share of the daily chores, and promising Hannah that before the heavy snows came, he'd repair the leaky roof and fill the cracks between the cabin logs with fresh mud so everyone would keep dry all winter.

As he listened, Drifter focused his attention on Drew – which not only took his mind off Hannah, but allowed him to mull over the consequences facing him if he stayed and helped Drew with the repairs. It was a tough choice. But finally, loyalty to Drew overcame Drifter's lust for Hannah and he decided to stay. Before he could tell Drew, though, Hannah responded to her husband's promise by grasping his hand and speaking softly to him.

Drifter didn't hear what she said. But he could tell by both their expressions that it was loving and heart-felt.

At once, Drifter's conscience again reminded him of his feelings for Hannah, and urged him to ride on. Simultaneously, he felt jealous of Drew. He immediately chided himself, knowing he had no right to be jealous of a man for loving his wife.

But before he could decide what to do, destiny over-ruled Drifter's integrity. As he searched his mind for the least hurtful way to tell Drew he was leaving, he heard horses rein up outside.

'See who it is, would you, please?' Drew told Lydon.

She ran to the window and looked out. 'It's, uh, Mr Stadtlander's son, Slade.'

'Who's with him?'

'The Iverson brothers . . . and a bunch of Double-S riders.'

Drew grimly eyed Drifter. 'That can only mean one thing.'

Drifter nodded. Rising, he buckled on his gun-belt while Drew grabbed the Winchester from above the door.

'Wait, wait!' Hannah exclaimed. 'Please, both of you – don't go looking for trouble. At least find out why they're here before. . . .'

Drew cut her off. 'Let's not fool ourselves, woman. There's only one reason for them to be here, and it surely ain't to wish us a merry Christmas!'

'Maybe not. But . . .'

'Enough, Hannah! Every day for months now, we've been expecting trouble. Now that it's here, at our front door, there's no way we can sidestep it. Our only chance of survival is to face it head on, and then maybe – just maybe – Old Man Stadtlander will get it through his thick head that we ain't moving or backing down, and will call off his dogs.'

'And if you get killed?' Hannah demanded. 'What happens to Lydon and me?'

'I promise you, woman, I ain't going to get killed!'

'You *hope* you're not, you mean?'

'Hannah, please, now's not the time to argue with me! You and Lydon just stay here, indoors, and don't – I repeat, *don't* – come out for any reason! Is that clear?'

'Crystal,' Hannah said, admiring his courage.

'Same goes for you,' Drew told Drifter. 'I appreciate that you're willing to throw in with me, Quint, but this ain't your fight. It's mine! And if I'm ever going to make Old Man Stadtlander realize he can't push me around, I got to handle his buzzards on my own.'

'Fair enough,' Drifter said. 'All the same, *compadre*, I'm coming out. Not for you or your family,' he added as Drew started to protest. 'but for myself. I got me a personal score to settle with this scum – especially Slade!'

'All right,' Drew said grudgingly. 'But do me one favor, will you?'

'Ask.'

'Let me throw the first horseshoe, OK?'

'Got my word on it, *amigo*.'

Satisfied, Drew led Drifter to the door. There he paused, took a deep breath to compose himself, and opened it. Then together, the two men stepped out into the damp, chilling morning light.

CHAPTER FOURTEEN

Outside, Slade and the Iverson brothers had looped their ropes around the corral gate and were backing up their horses. As the ropes grew taut, the gate and one of its posts were ripped out of the ground. The other gunmen hooted and hollered and fired their rifles in the air. The shots panicked some unbroken mustangs locked in the corral. Nickering with fear, they ran fearfully in circles and then finally came charging out through the broken gate.

Drew ran forward, arms extended, and tried to block the escaping mustangs. But it was useless. The terrified horses raced past on either side of him and galloped off into the open desert.

Laughing among themselves, Slade, Mace, Cory and the gunmen reined up in front of Drew and Drifter.

'I got a message for you, sodbuster,' Slade told Drew. 'My old man says you got until the end of the week to clear out. Lock, stock and barrel. Otherwise, we'll be back. And next time, I promise you we won't be so gentle. We'll burn the whole damned place down around you and your family! You hear me, dirt farmer?'

'Loud and clear,' Drew said. 'Now, you hear me. Ride back to your father and tell him that I ain't moving. Not now. Not tomorrow. Not ever. I own this land, fair and legal, and what's more, I got the deed to prove it. . . .'

'*Deed?*' Slade echoed. He laughed derisively and turned to the other men. 'Did you hear that, boys? Mr Dirt Farmer here, says he's got a *deed*!'

Mace, Cory and the gunmen hooted mockingly.

'Now, you listen up, sodbuster,' Slade snarled at Drew. 'This so-called deed you're talking about, hell, it ain't worth the stinking paper it's written on!'

'And even if it was,' Mace chimed in, 'it ain't going to do you no good. Not when you're six feet under.'

'My brother's right,' Cory added. 'What's more, that don't hold true just for you. The same goes for all the other dirt-grubbing farmers plowing up this valley.'

'The hell it does!' Drew said, glaring at Slade. 'You and your gunmen might get away with shooting some of us, but not even the mighty Stillman J. Stadtlander can justify killing everyone without bringing the law down on his head!'

'Law?' Slade scoffed. 'What law? My old man's the only law around here. He bought off that dimwit sheriff years ago. And everyone knows it. But go ahead. You and all your other sodbuster pals can wave your deeds around till the moon turns green. It ain't going to matter none. Not to my pa. Far as he's concerned, anything you say will just go in one ear and out the other!'

Drifter, silent until now, turned to Drew. 'What'd I tell you, *compadre*? It's like I been saying all along: Old Man Stadtlander may be rich and powerful, but he's got nothing 'tween his ears but hot air!'

'Mister,' Slade angrily warned Drifter, 'if you want to keep on breathing, you best keep your damned mouth shut!'

'And if I don't? What then?'

Slade paled, teeth gritted, itching to draw but too yellow to try it.

'Figures,' Drifter mocked. 'You're no different than the rest of your misfit crew – gutless to the core!'

For a moment no one moved.

Then a bearded, ginger-haired gunman named Big 'Red' Gelson nudged his horse forward and confronted Drifter. 'Care to repeat that, mister?'

'Why?' Drifter said. 'You deaf as well as pig ugly?'

'Damn you!' Gelson snarled and grabbed for his six-gun.

So did Drifter. His gun-hand blurred. Suddenly, almost magically, his pistol appeared in his fist. He fired, once, from the hip, and the bullet punched a neat hole in Gelson's forehead. Momentarily, the gunman looked shocked, as if he couldn't believe he was dead, then he slumped forward, slid from his saddle and fell on to the dirt.

Drifter holstered his pistol and faced Slade and the

other gunmen. 'How about it?' he taunted. 'Any of you jokers feeling lucky?'

No one moved. No one spoke. It was silent save for the softly moaning wind.

'What's the matter, sonny?' Drifter asked Slade. 'Your blood turn to piss all of a sudden?'

Slade reddened with rage and shame. Desperate to draw, his gun-hand twitched. But at the same time fear gripped him, preventing him from reaching for his gun.

'Like father, like son,' Drifter mocked. 'Blowhards, both of you!' He turned to the Iversons and the other gunmen, adding: 'Don't *none* of you got any guts?'

'I do,' a voice lisped quietly.

Drifter and everyone else turned and looked at the small, slim, immaculately dressed man who had just stepped out from behind the cabin.

'So, why don't you try me, gunny?'

'Be happy to,' Drifter said. As he spoke, he kept his eye on Clay Hudson's left hand, remembering that the gunman's left holster was more worn than his right. 'Go ahead, shorty. Call it.'

Clay Hudson tensed, his eyes two ice-blue slits, gloved hands poised above his holstered six-guns.

Drifter, sensing Hudson wasn't bluffing, knew he'd have to be at his best in order to out-draw the little gunman.

'Stop it, damn it – both of you!' Hannah stepped out of the cabin, holding an old scattergun that she aimed at Clay Hudson and the Iverson brothers. 'There's been more than enough killing already. So unless one of you wants to be the next corpse, pick up your dead and ride out of here!' As if to convince everyone, she cocked back both hammers, adding: 'And I do mean *now*!'

CHAPTER FIFTEEN

Once Slade, Clay, the Iverson brothers and the gunmen had ridden off, Hannah lowered the shotgun and pointed at the blood reddening the ground in front of Drifter and her husband.

'I'd be obliged if one of you would clean that up. Lydon's already seen too much blood for her years. She doesn't need to play in it.'

'I'll take care of it right away,' Drew promised.

There was an edge to his voice, and Hannah, guessing why, said: 'I'm sorry for not obeying you, honey. But I couldn't stand by and watch you shoot it out with professional gunmen. You could've been killed. And Lydon and me, we need you too much to let that happen.'

'I need you two just as much,' Drew said, softened by her concern. 'If I didn't, I wouldn't have told you to stay inside. But now. . . .'

'Go on,' Hannah urged as he paused. 'We have no secrets from each other.'

'I was just thinking about Old Man Stadtlander.'

'What about him?'

'Well, now that he's finally showed his hand, he ain't going to stop. From now on, he's going to keep sending Slade and his gunmen to harass us – maybe worse.'

'You mean he might kill us?' broke in Lydon.

'Be quiet,' her mother snapped. Then to Drew: 'That's a pleasant thought.'

'The truth ain't always pleasant, Hannah. We both know that.'

'So what do you suggest?'

'I'm not sure. But I was wondering . . .' He broke off, as if not wanting to hear what he was going to say, then said it anyway: 'Now that there's been a killing and one of his gunmen are dead, well, that raises the stakes and. . . .'

'And?'

'Well, much as I love this grubby little patch of dirt, I got to ask myself: is it really worth risking our lives for?' He paused, and this time looked at Drifter as if needing an answer.

The tall, taciturn gunfighter shrugged. 'Reckon that's something only you and Hannah can decide, *compadre*.'

'I know, but . . . what if you were me, Quint, would you stay?'

Drifter stood there, stoically silent.

'You're asking the wrong man,' Hannah told Drew. 'He's not called Drifter because he dreams of settling down.'

'Your wife's right,' Drifter agreed. 'I'm the last fella you should be asking, *amigo*. Hell, I ain't nothing more than a wandering gun. Always will be.'

'Not if you were to accept my offer and hunker down here, with us,' Drew said. 'Or are you determined to ride on, no matter what?'

Drifter glanced at Hannah, saw disappointment chasing all hope from her green eyes, and couldn't bring himself to answer Drew's question.

Encouraged by his silence, Hannah said: 'It wouldn't have to be for long, Quint. Just long enough to help my husband finish those repairs I mentioned.'

'Whoa,' Drew said, surprised. 'I didn't know you two had discussed. . . .'

'Mother,' Lydon blurted, 'can I say something?'

Hannah glared at her daughter. 'What've I told you about interrupting?'

'Please, momma. It's real important.'

'If it's important,' Drew said to Hannah, 'I'd like to hear what it is.'

'Very well,' she said. Then to Lydon: 'Go ahead. But make it quick.'

Lydon turned and gazed up at Drifter. 'I know this ain't none of my business. And you don't have to answer me if you don't want to. But since you're the one who brought it up in the first place. . . .'

'Brought what up?'

'How far the sorrel had brung you. And how wore out he was, and . . . how much he needed to be rested up. Remember?'

'Lydon . . .' Hannah began.

Drifter raised his hand, stopping her. 'No, she's right. I did say that. What's more, she's right about the sorrel. Chances are, I could ruin a fine horse if I don't rest him for a few more days.'

79

'Then there's your reason,' Drew insisted.

'Reason?'

'For accepting my offer.'

Drifter hesitated, met Hannah's eyes, saw renewed hope in them and knew he was beaten.

'Fair enough,' he told Drew. 'I'll stick around for a spell.'

Lydon's face lit up excitedly, and she had to clasp both hands over her mouth in order to stifle her joyful whoop.

CHAPTER SIXTEEN

It was mid-morning a few days later and the hot sun beat mercilessly down on Drifter as he packed handfuls of wet mud into the chinks between the logs of the cabin walls. He was hatless, stripped to the waist, and had mud all over his sweaty, muscular upper body. Nearby sat a half-full bucket of fresh mud while a second bucket, holding only water, cast a long shadow on to the trough.

He was working alone. But behind him in a fenced field, Drew could be seen limping behind a horse-drawn plow. Reins draped over his shoulders, he guided the sharp blade so that it dug straight furrows in the dry, reddish-brown earth.

Drifter finished packing a handful of mud between two upper logs on the east wall, and then paused to back-hand the sweat from his brow. As he did, he glanced toward the barn. Inside, through the open door, he could see Hannah churning buttermilk. Beside her, Lydon sat on a bale of hay, glumly studying a school book. She looked bored and restless, and eagerly looked up when her mother stopped churning

81

to speak to her. Drifter couldn't hear what Hannah was saying, but as he continued to watch, he saw her fill a tin mug with buttermilk, hold it out to her daughter and point toward Drew.

Lydon gladly set her book down and came trotting out of the barn, mug in hand.

'Careful,' Hannah called after her. 'Don't spill it all before you get there.' About to continue churning, she noticed Drifter watching her. She beckoned to him, indicated the tall wooden bucket containing the churned buttermilk and pretended to drink from a glass.

Drifter waved to show he understood, wiped the mud from his hands on his pants, and started for the barn. On the way he passed Lydon. She smirked at him, as if they shared a sinful secret, and then hurried on.

Irked at himself for letting a young girl get under his skin, Drifter entered the barn and joined Hannah. She'd already filled another mug with buttermilk and now offered it to him, saying: 'It's not as cool as I'd like, but it'll help quench your thirst.'

'Thanks . . .' Drifter took a long gulp of lukewarm buttermilk, felt it glide pleasantly down his throat and instantly felt refreshed.

'More?' Hannah asked when he'd drained the mug.

'Uh-uh. That hit the spot.' He handed her the mug and turned to leave.

'Wait.'

Then as Drifter stopped and turned back to her:

'I shouldn't ask you this, but . . . I have to know something.'

Curious, Drifter waited for her to continue.

82

Hannah hesitated, licked the buttermilk off one thumb, and then candidly said: 'Are you . . . uhm . . . glad you didn't ride on?'

'Sure. Why? Shouldn't I be?'

'Y-yes, of course! I . . . I didn't . . . mean it like that, Quint. What I meant was . . . oh, darn it, I don't know what I meant. I just needed to know.'

Drifter smiled, and said 'Fair enough', and in his mind started to walk away. But in fact he just stood there, gazing at Hannah without realizing it.

There was a brief silence . . . finally broken by the sorrel nickering in its stall.

The sound interrupted Drifter's thoughts. He'd been thinking of all the things he wanted to tell Hannah but couldn't without betraying his integrity. Now, brought back to reality by the restless sorrel, he said: 'Well, reckon I should get. . . .'

'Yes, yes, of course,' Hannah interrupted, 'Get back to work before the mud dries. I know that. But it's just . . . well, before you go, I must tell you something.'

'I'm listening.'

'What you did was a truly unselfish thing – for Drew, I mean. Especially since I know deep down you wanted to ride on. But you didn't. You stayed to help Drew, and honestly, I must tell you that it's made all the difference to him. And for that, Quint, I can't thank you enough.'

'No thanks needed,' Drifter said, fighting the urge to crush her against him. 'Being around you folks has given me more pleasure than I've known in quite a spell. . . .'

'Has it?' Hannah said, desperately wanting to believe him. 'I mean, has it really, Quint?'

'More than I can describe.'

'You're not just saying that because it's the correct thing to say?'

Drifter laughed hollowly. 'Being correct, Hannah, ain't exactly high on my list.'

'It isn't? How odd. I would've thought it, well, you know, it was. . . .'

Drifter reached out a mud-caked hand and gently tilted her face up so that she looked directly into his eyes.

'Reckon you don't know me as well as I figured, Hannah, otherwise you'd never even think of asking me something like that.'

'I wouldn't?'

'Not if you were thinking straight.'

'I suppose not . . .' Hannah reddened with embarrassment. 'Well, I guess my only excuse is that I'm having such a hard time keeping away from you, it's affecting my sanity. Oh, my God,' she blurted, hand clasped over her mouth. 'I can't believe I actually said that. It sounds so dramatic . . . so . . . so school-girlish!'

Drifter didn't say anything. Her words summed up his own feelings so well, he couldn't find anything suitable to add.

Hannah, as if reading his thoughts, said: 'It's so hard, I swear at times it actually hurts.'

Drifter nodded in silent, painful agreement.

'What I can't figure out, is, when it gets to be more than a person can take, what do you do then to keep your emotions in check?'

Drifter shrugged. 'Well, I don't know about you, but me? I think of Drew.'

'In what way?'

'I remind myself what a fine, moral man he is, and how rock-bottom lousy I'd feel if I betrayed his trust. What?' Drifter added when Hannah looked sidelong at him. 'You don't think gunfighters can have a sense of honor?'

'I've never known a gunfighter before, Quint, so I have no one to compare you to.' She paused, searching her heart for answers, then said: 'But I do know this: much as I love Drew, I can't tell you the number of times throughout the day that every part of me hungers for you. What's worse, is the knowledge that deep down, where, as my father used to say, the truth and lying never stop fighting each other, I know that all you'd have to do is snap your fingers and, so help me Satan, I'd ride off with you to hell and back! And if you can make any sense out of that, Quint Longley,' she concluded disgustedly, 'then please, by all means, do so.'

'I can't, Hannah. I honestly can't.'

She wasn't listening. 'I've gone over it in my head a hundred times and the answer's always the same: it can't be love. It's too soon for that – isn't it? Surely, you can't just instantly love someone you barely know? Can you? I mean, it isn't rational.' She paused and shook her head, as if arguing with herself inside, then said: 'But when I asked myself, what was the alternative, the only answer I could come up with was lust, and the thought of that made me ashamed. My God, I'm no puritan, but neither was I ever a wanton woman. So all

I can assume is that I was attracted to you, Quint, because you're everything Drew isn't, and could never be.'

Drifter struggled to find words to ease both their pain. It wasn't easy. But finally, he said: 'Maybe we should leave it at that.'

'I couldn't agree more.' She paused, questioning herself, then said: 'I don't have many sterling qualities, Quint, and I'm aware of that. Thanks to my father, who worshipped the ground I trod on, I was spoiled growing up and got used to getting my way. But despite that, I've always tried to tell the truth, even when it wasn't in my best interest . . .' She broke off as Lydon came running into the barn.

'Momma! Momma!'

'What is it, sweetheart?' Hannah asked, concerned.

'It's Pa Drew,' Lydon said breathlessly.

'What about him?'

'H-he went and broke it!'

'Broke what?'

'The plow blade!'

CHAPTER SEVENTEEN

Anxious to get the blade fixed as soon as possible, Drew had Drifter help him load the heavy, cumbersome old plow on to the wagon. Then together they hitched up the team and prepared to drive into town.

Against Drew's wishes, Hannah insisted on accompanying them. She'd been secretly saving her pennies for months in hopes of buying a new dress, and though she hadn't intended to go into town until Christmas, she wasn't about to let this unexpected opportunity pass her by.

Neither was Lydon. For weeks she'd been grumbling about how sick she was of reading schoolbooks, and now, rather than miss the excitement of a trip into town, she was willing to wash up, brush her hair and even wear a 'silly dress and shoes!'

Drifter, knowing that he might run into Slade and the Iversons, or even Clay Hudson, buckled on his gun-belt and grabbed his Winchester from the saddle scabbard. Then, making sure both guns were fully loaded, he left the barn and joined the Albrights at the wagon.

At first, he'd planned on riding his horse. But then, still worried that his feelings for Hannah might eventually force him to leave, Drifter decided to give the sorrel another day of rest and climbed on to the driver's seat next to Drew.

Though it was not an overly long ride into town, the broiling desert sun made it almost unbearable. It didn't help that there was no wind and only a few tiny clouds. As a result, the intense, almost suffocating heat seemed to bounce off the parched ground, searing their faces.

Drew, not wanting to wear out the horses, drove more slowly than normal. As a result, by the time they'd reached the blacksmith shop at the edge of town, sweat was pouring off everyone, draining them of energy.

As the four of them climbed down from the wagon, they heard the blacksmith hammering on his anvil at the rear of the shop. Drew, tired of listening to Lydon begging for a soda, gave her a nickel and promised Hannah that he and Drifter would join them at the ice-cream parlor as soon as he'd talked to the black-smith.

Hannah was more than happy to oblige, knowing it would give her extra time to look at dresses. Pecking Drew fondly on the cheek and with Lydon in tow, she headed for Front Street. Drew watched them leave, and then joined Drifter at the back of the wagon. Together they wrestled the heavy old plow down on to the ground and dragged it into the shop.

Inside they found the blacksmith, a hulking, powerful, dedicated Mormon named Thaddius McClory, working by his furnace. When he'd finished hammering, he used a pair of blackened tongs to pick up a broken wagon axle and dip its white-hot tip into a barrel of water. The metal hissed and clouds of steam rose around him. He waited a few seconds, then withdrew the now-cooled axle from the water and set it on his bench.

'Looks to me,' Drew grinned as he and Drifter joined the blacksmith, 'that we've caught you right when you got nothing to do.'

Thaddius chuckled, 'Amen to that, brother,' and wiped the sweat from his brow with a massive hairy forearm. 'But, like my dear old papa was fond of saying: "Hard work is an honest man's path to heaven."'

'I knew there was a reason I was going to hell,' Drifter joked.

Thaddius wasn't amused. He scowled at Drifter, said something disparaging under his breath, then wiped away more sweat before asking Drew: 'What can I do for you, Brother Albright?'

'The blade of my plow's broken and I need you to fix it right away.'

'And by God, I'd surely like to accommodate you,' Thaddius said sincerely. 'But as you can see, I'm already swamped with work and, well, truth is, I won't be able to repair it until the end of next week, earliest.'

Drew sighed unhappily: 'A wait like that could cost me my farm, Thad.'

'I'm sorry to hear that, Brother Albright, but facts is facts. . . .'

'I know that, Thad, but surely there's some way you could fit me in sooner?'

'I fear not.'

Drifter now turned to Drew, saying: 'Reckon you should be going, *amigo*.'

'G-going?'

'Sure. You promised to meet Hannah and Lydon at the ice-cream parlor, remember?'

'I know, but. . . .'

'So, keep your word, *compadre*. Otherwise they'll be mighty disappointed.'

Drew, about to protest, saw a look in Drifter's gray eyes that warned him not to argue. 'O-oh, yeah,' he exclaimed, 'ice-cream parlor, of course! I forgot all about promising to meet them there. Thanks for reminding me, Quint. Good day, Thad.' He hurried off before the surprised blacksmith could say anything.

'What on earth come over him all of a sudden?' McClory asked Drifter.

'He gets squeamish at the sight of blood.'

'Blood? What bloo. . . ?' Thaddius stopped abruptly as he felt Drifter's Bowie knife dig into his belly.

'Why, yours, of course,' Drifter said. Then as the blacksmith's eyes bulged: 'Now, why don't you be the good Mormon you pretend to be and fix that blade? I'll pay your price, so long as it's fair, and then get out of your hair. But I warn you, *Brother* McClory, just as sure as I'm going to hell, your life depends on that blade being ready when Drew and I return.'

CHAPTER EIGHTEEN

As Drifter crossed the street and headed for Melvin's haberdashery store, a young, gaunt-faced gunman named Hal Fermin pushed out through the batwing doors of the Copper Palace. He was grinning about a joke he'd just been told, but on seeing Drifter he lost his grin, and alarmed, quickly ducked back into the saloon. He stood there, heart thudding, cautiously peering over the batwing doors, watching as Drifter stepped on to the boardwalk and entered the store.

Fermin sagged with relief. Despite being one of Stadtlander's hired guns, he knew he was no match for the tall, deadly gunfighter and continued to stand there, peering over the batwing doors, until he was sure that Drifter wasn't coming out. Then he left the saloon and hurried to his horse that was tied to a nearby hitching rail. Untying a blue roan that had Stadtlander's Double-S brand on its rump, he swung up into the saddle, wheeled the horse around and galloped out of town.

Drifter, who had been watching Fermin through the store window, now turned and walked over to

Drew, Hannah and Lydon who stood in a line of customers at the recently built soda fountain. Ice cream was new to the southwest, but thanks to Melvin, who'd taken a financial risk by bringing it to Santa Rosa, it had quickly become popular. Daily, Melvin happily listened as the cash register rang up sales, all the time quietly congratulating himself for making his store the envy of the territory. He had to admit, though, it had been costly. He'd not only had to build an ice house in which to store the large quantities of ice and rock salt needed to make ice cream, but had been forced to travel to St Louis to purchase an ice-cream maker – a new-fangled machine, comprised of twin stirring paddles inserted inside each of the two cylindrical containers that held all the necessary chemicals.

But it had been worth it. And now, as Melvin stood watching Drifter, Drew, Hannah, Lydon and the other customers licking their ice-cream cones, he knew his foresight had paid off, and gleefully rubbed his hands together.

Hannah, unaware she was being watched, teased Lydon about having ice cream on the tip of her nose and then turned to Drifter, saying: 'Drew mentioned you two had trouble convincing Mr McClory to fix the plow blade today. . . .'

'I told Hannah how busy he was filling previous orders,' Drew put in quickly.

'Yeah,' Drifter said. 'Or so he claimed.'

'You think he was lying?' Hannah said.

'Lying's a harsh word, ma'am, and one I try not to pin on a fella. I'd sooner say that McClory was . . . well, just trying to hike up the price.'

'And were you able to make him change his mind and help us?'

'Sure. After we pow-wowed for a spell.'

Hannah laughed. 'How much extra did your pow-wow cost?'

'Not a red cent.'

'Really? How'd you manage that?'

'Negotiation,' Drifter said drily. He crunched down the last of his ice-cream cone before adding: 'Truth is, McClory ain't a bad sort at heart. And once I made him understand how important it was for Drew to get the blade fixed right away, heck, he was more than happy to oblige. He even promised to have it finished by the time we head home. . . .'

Drifter broke off as out of the corner of his eye he saw Lars enter. Pausing by the door, the crippled stableman leaned on his pitchfork and look around. Then on seeing Drifter, he came limping toward him.

Drifter, noticing how agitated Lars looked, excused himself, and went to meet him before he could reach the soda fountain counter.

'*Qué pasa, compadre?*'

'Well, I could be mistook, bucko, but I overheard some folks saying that Clay Hudson's in town and he's looking for you. And I don't mean in a sociable way.'

'Where is he, do you know?'

'Copper Palace. Playing poker.'

'Thanks,' Drifter said. 'Reckon I'll go make it easy for him.'

'Figured that's what you'd say.'

'That don't sit right with you?'

'I wouldn't say that, exactly.'

93

'What, then, *compadre*?'

Lars hesitated and sucked his gums, a sure sign he was concerned.

'You don't think I can beat him?' Drifter said. 'Is that what's worrying you?'

'Well . . . word is, he's plenty fast.'

'So, you figure I'd be better off saddling up my sorrel at Drew's place and make myself scarce?'

'Never said that.'

'But it's what you meant, right?'

'No, that ain't so,' Lars said. 'Truth is, only reason I came here was to remind you that you *do* have that option. I'll even loan you a bronc to ride out to Drew's and get your own pony, if that's what you decide.'

'Fair enough,' Drifter said. 'Anything else?'

'Nope.' Lars fondly squeezed Drifter's arm, 'See you around, bucko,' then turned and with the help of the pitchfork limped out of the store.

Drifter, mind racing, heard someone approaching from behind. He whirled around, hand dropping to his pistol, and then relaxed as he saw it was Drew.

'Something wrong, Quint?'

'Nah,' Drifter said. 'Lars just reminded me that I got business to attend to.'

'Want me to go with you?'

'No, thanks. But come to think of it, *amigo*, I reckon it'd be smart if you and your family was to head on over to McClory's place and see if he's got your plow blade fixed.'

'In other words,' Drew said, reading Drifter's tight-lipped expression, 'don't hang around town any longer than we have to?'

'Sums it up.'

'And you? After you finish your . . . uhm . . . "business", how will you get to my place? Your sorrel's still in the barn, remember?'

'Sure. Won't be a problem. I can borrow a bronc from Lars, if I need one.'

'Then I'll see you soon, partner . . .' Drew stuck out his hand.

Drifter shook it warmly, and with a touch of sadness. 'You bet, *compadre.*' As he spoke, he glanced over Drew's shoulder at Hannah. She was talking to Lydon and didn't see him looking at her. He sighed longingly, gave Drew a throwaway salute and walked out of the store.

Drew stared after him for several moments. '*Buena suerte, mí amigo,*' he said, fondly. He then reined in his emotions, and returned to Hannah and Lydon.

CHAPTER NINETEEN

Lars Gustafson was right: Clay Hudson was in the old decaying Copper Palace playing poker at the main table. Due to an unlucky run of poor cards, he'd lost the last few hands and was growing more and more frustrated. The other players, aware of his mean streak, were careful not to say anything to antagonize him.

Drifter now pushed in through the squeaking batwing doors, paused and looked around. On seeing Clay, he rested his right hand on the butt of his holstered pistol and approached the little gunman with slow, purposeful steps.

If Clay saw Drifter coming, he didn't show it. He just kept studying his cards as if his life depended upon it.

But the other card players saw Drifter, and alarmed by his grim, tight-lipped expression, they froze.

Drifter ignored them and kept his eyes fixed on Clay.

A man drinking at the bar noticed the fear on the card players' faces and spread the word to his fellow drinkers. They all quickly backed up out of the line of fire. Tension spread throughout the saloon. It grew so quiet a moth could be heard beating its wings against the glass of one of the kerosene lamps.

On reaching the table, Drifter stopped in front of Clay, and said quietly: 'Hear you're looking for me, Hudson?'

Clay looked up and smiled as if he'd just been dealt a straight flush. 'Yeth.'

'Well, now you've found me.'

'True,' Clay lisped. 'Thweet of you to thave me the trouble.'

'Pleasure's all mine,' Drifter said mockingly. 'Though I shouldn't take credit. See, this dwarf I once knew told me how much it hurt his feet to walk in elevated heels, so I figured I'd spare *you* some pain.'

Clay smiled, as if amused by Drifter's taunting. But rage narrowed his ice-blue eyes, and placing his cards face down on the green felt-covered table, he stood up.

Alarmed, the other players jumped up and scrambled out of the line of fire.

The men drinking at the bar did the same, scattering like scared mice.

Clay kicked his chair aside and glared at Drifter, who towered above him.

'You may not know it, gunny,' he lisped, 'but you juth reached the end of the trail. And thith time, there ain't a woman or a deputy with a thotgun to thave you.'

'Lucky me.'

'Won't be no th-theriff to cold-cock me from behind, neither.'

'Fair enough,' Drifter said. 'Now, are you going to draw that smoke-cannon of yours, or talk me to death?'

Stung, Clay tensed like a coiled spring, hands hovering above his holstered guns.

Drifter concentrated on the gunman's left hand, knowing it would move first.

'I'm still waiting – *Shorty.*'

It was the final insult. And it goaded Clay into action.

But an instant before either he or Drifter could draw, Nature interfered.

An earthquake struck.

Though the epicenter was several miles away in the Rio Grande valley – a vast seismic region known as the rift – the quake was powerful enough to shake the entire town of Santa Rosa – including the Copper Palace.

The saloon floor abruptly heaved upward, parts of it splitting into ever-widening cracks, while the whole building began to shake with nightmarish violence.

Furniture toppled over. The upright piano overturned, crushing the old piano player, and then slid across the floor, injuring anyone else it struck.

Everyone, including Drifter and Clay, was thrown off their feet.

Many were hit by sliding furniture, and, dazed, rolled helplessly across the still heaving floor.

The stairs to the second floor swayed and buckled but somehow didn't break.

Muffled screams of terror came from the whores servicing men in their rooms.

Liquor bottles flew off the long back bar and smashed wherever they landed.

The huge mirror that covered the wall behind the bar shattered, the sharp jagged pieces stabbing numerous customers like flying daggers.

The big glass chandelier swung wildly from side to side, finally ripping itself loose from the ceiling and crashing down on the people below.

Everybody panicked and desperately scrambled for the door.

Then, just as quickly as the quake started, it ended.

The ground suddenly stopped shaking and became still.

The old, badly damaged saloon creaked ominously for several moments, then grew deafeningly quiet.

No one moved. They scarcely breathed.

Drifter pushed aside the broken furniture piled atop him. His heart pounded in his throat and blood ran from a gash on his forehead, but otherwise he was unhurt.

Others weren't so lucky. Part of the roof had caved in, and the broken beams had crashed down on many of the customers. They lay everywhere, painful moans and groans coming from the injured.

Drifter slowly got to his knees and looked around for Clay Hudson. But the little gunfighter was nowhere to be seen. Rising, Drifter steadied himself, and then on wobbly legs stepped over the piles of broken beams and furniture and joined several men who were helping to drag injured customers out of the debris.

But Nature wasn't finished. Within minutes the

aftershock hit.

The ground trembled briefly, alarming everyone, and then became still.

The earthquake that one day in the future would become part of New Mexico's history was finally over.

The Copper Palace was not the only damaged building in Santa Rosa. Most of the stores, offices and other saloons in town suffered some form of damage, but because they were smaller, single-storey and not as old, they remained standing and no one inside was seriously hurt.

The townspeople who weren't injured worked tirelessly to help those who were. Drifter and Lars pitched in, helping to assist the men, women and children who couldn't walk to the infirmary or the nearest doctor's office. It was back-breaking work, and by the time dusk fell, they were exhausted. By now, most of the population was gradually trying to get their lives back to normal, and Drifter and Lars, satisfied they'd done enough, wearily entered the undamaged livery stable.

Inside, they enjoyed a few swigs from a fresh bottle of rye over a dish of cold leftovers. Then Drifter, energy somewhat restored, waited while the old stableman saddled up a big rangy chestnut with four white stockings that was built to run forever. A year ago, Lars had traded an old saddle and a Remington bolt-action rifle for the then new Colt, and at the time figured he'd gotten the best of the deal. But as the handsome stallion matured, Lars soon discovered that good looks and speed came at a price: the horse was not only skittish and tried to cow-kick anyone who got close, but it bucked without warning, unseating all but the most experienced riders.

Fortunately, Drifter rode as if he'd been born in the saddle, and Lars confidently handed the tall gunfighter the reins without even asking him when he'd return the edgy stallion.

Instead, he said: 'Any word on Clay Hudson?'

Drifter shook his head and stepped up into the saddle.

'Did you check with the coroner or the doctor?'

'Just the coroner. The doc's swamped with injured patients.'

'So there's a good chance Hudson's still alive?'

'Only time will tell.'

'I reckon so. By the way, bucko, after you pick up your sorrel at Drew's, where you figure on heading?'

'I ain't given it no thought. Why? D'you need your horse back right away?'

'No. Next time Drew comes to town will be fine.'

'Fair enough.' Drifter leaned down and fondly shook hands with his friend, '*Adiós, compadre*,' and rode out of the livery stable.

Lars stared after Drifter until he could no longer hear the chestnut's hoofbeats. Then he muttered, 'Keep him safe, Lord,' and with the help of the pitch-fork, limped to the rain barrel. There, he pulled out a fresh bottle of whiskey and took a long, satisfying gulp.

CHAPTER TWENTY

When Drifter reached the outskirts of town, he saw
riders approaching in the distance. Though they were
still too far away for him to recognize, he sensed something ominous about them, and, ever cautious, rode
behind a rocky outcrop alongside the trail. There he
reined in the chestnut, pulled his Winchester from the
scabbard and levered in a round.

Watched.

Waited.

Soon the riders came close enough for Drifter to
see their faces. He immediately recognized them as
Stadtlander's hired gunmen. They were led by Slade,
while beside him rode the Iverson brothers and Hal
Fermin.

Drifter waited until the horsemen were almost level
with him and then rode out onto the trail in front of
them.

Startled, the riders quickly reined up, their horses
jostling together in confusion.

Drifter kept his rifle aimed at Slade as he said
grimly: 'Looking for me, sonny?'

Though alarmed, Slade tried to hide his fear behind a mask of belligerence. 'If you want to keep living, Longley,' he warned, 'better put up that rifle.'

Drifter laughed mockingly. 'Just like your pa – full of threats you can't deliver.'

Slade turned white with rage. 'Damn you! Leave my father out of this, or. . . .'

'Or what, sonny? You'll gun me down?' Drifter tucked the Winchester back into the scabbard and dropped his hand to his Colt. 'Well, here's your chance.'

Slade's gun-hand tensed, but though tempted, he didn't draw.

'Go ahead,' Drifter taunted. 'You're always bragging about how fast you are. So, prove it. What's the problem?' he added when Slade didn't move. 'Why don't you back up that big mouth of yours for once?'

Momentarily, Slade became so enraged that it seemed as if he might do as Drifter dared. But then his yellow streak kicked in and inwardly he crumbled.

'You got the drop on me this time,' he said lamely. 'But I ain't worried. There's always tomorrow.'

Drifter grinned wolfishly. 'Last fella that said that to me was Clay Hudson. And he's gone missing.'

'So what?' Slade sneered. 'Clay don't mean nothing to me.'

'He should. You hired him to kill me.'

'That ain't true. It was my old man who hired him.'

'That's a lie. And if you weren't such a sniveling weasel, you'd admit it.'

Slade gave a forced laugh. 'Go ahead. Insult me all you like. You're just wasting your breath. Nothing you can say is going to prod me into jerking my iron against you. I ain't *that* loco.'

'Too bad,' Drifter said, adding: 'Reckon I was wrong about you, sonny. You do have some brains after all.'

'Enough to know that after today, this whole territory won't be big enough to hide you – not now that my old man's sworn to see you dangling from a rope!'

'I hope he's a patient man.'

'Why?'

' 'Cause there's a whole bushel of folks lined up ahead of him, all with the same intentions, and none of them has been successful yet.'

'That's 'cause they ain't my old man,' Slade bragged. 'Nothing deters him. Hell, he'll just put a price on your head that's big enough to entice every lawman, bounty hunter and one-eyed dog-catcher in the Southwest to hunt you down. Trust me, Longley, your days are numbered!'

'Could be you're right,' Drifter admitted. ' 'Course, either way the outcome won't matter to you, sonny.'

'Meaning?'

'You won't get to watch. You'll be six feet under!' Though he spoke barely above a whisper, the menace in Drifter's voice was so frightening that Slade's mouth went dry.

'Y-you kill me,' he stammered, 'and it'll be murder, plain and simple.'

'How you figure that?'

'Because, like I just told you, ain't nothing you can say that'll make me draw against you.'

'Figures,' Drifter said scornfully. 'Like all bullies,

104

you're yellow to the bone. But you needn't sweat it, sonny. I ain't fixing to kill you. We're just going to take a little ride together.'

Slade, alarmed by the idea, tried to hide his fear behind a defiant sneer. 'Now I know you're loco. Either that or you been smoking too much opium over at the Chinaman's.'

'Meaning?'

'I ain't going *nowhere* with you, Longley. What's more, if you try to force me, my men will fill you so full of lead your horse will collapse under the weight!'

'Why wait?' Cory Iverson chimed in. 'Let's shoot the bastard now!'

'Yeah, gun him down!' added his brother, Mace.

Ignoring their threats, Drifter drew his Colt with blurring speed and jammed the barrel against Slade's neck.

'Reckon I ain't making myself clear, sonny. So, I'll tell you again. I'm giving you a choice. Ride or die. It's your call.'

Slade anxiously bit his lip. Then unable to control his cowardliness, he told the Iversons and the gunmen: 'Keep your guns leathered, boys. I'm going with him.'

'Now you're making sense,' Drifter said. He grabbed the reins out of Slade's hands and wagged his pistol at the gunmen. 'Back up!'

'You heard him,' Slade barked when his men didn't move. 'Let us through!'

Grudgingly, the gunmen backed up their horses, letting Drifter and Slade pass.

'Hey, Slade,' Cody Iverson yelled. 'What should we

tell your old man? He's going to want to know where you are.'

Slade looked inquiringly at Drifter, who shrugged and said: 'So long as nobody follows us, you'll be home for supper.'

'You heard him,' Slade told the Iversons. 'Keep the hell out of this. You hear me?' he added to the gunmen. 'All of you, get back to the ranch!'

As one, the Iversons and the gunmen whirled their horses around and rode off across the open sun-burned desert.

CHAPTER TWENTY-ONE

Riding at a brisk pace, Drifter and Slade followed the meandering sandy trail that led to the Albrights' homestead. Neither man spoke. The only sounds came from the laboring horses, their jingling bits and the leathery squeak of the saddles under the men. But as the sun slowly dipped behind the distant hills, engulfing the desert in darkness, the night echoed with a chorus of mournful coyote howls.

When the two men neared the hills and could see lights burning in the windows of the Albrights' cabin, Drifter spurred the chestnut alongside Slade and told him to rein up. Slade obeyed, and at once began begging Drifter not to shoot him.

'No one's shooting anybody,' Drifter growled. 'So just quit yapping and listen carefully to what I'm going to tell you.'

'S-Sure, sure,' Slade whimpered. 'Anything you say.'

'You're free to go,' Drifter said. 'But I'm warning you, sonny. Cross me again, and I'll give the folks in

107

Santa Rosa something to celebrate – your funeral!'

Slade started to respond, but the menace in Drifter's narrowed gray eyes made him think better of it. And quickly wheeling his horse around, he spurred it in the direction of his father's ranch.

Drifter watched Slade riding away. 'I don't know why, horse,' he said, thinking aloud, 'but I got the damnedest feeling that letting that *hombre* go is going to come back to haunt me!'

Drifter spent the night bedded down in the hayloft of the Albright barn. He was dog tired, but before falling asleep, he promised himself that he would ride off in the morning. He didn't want to, in fact it was the last thing he wanted to do, but his integrity insisted. It also insisted that he never return. That way, he eliminated any chance of succumbing to his lust for Hannah, or, more importantly, destroying the respect that existed between himself and Drew.

It hurt him to think that he'd never see any of the Albrights again. Much to his surprise, he'd grown attached to both Drew and Lydon. Even so, Drifter knew he had no other choice. He *had* to ride on. . . .

What's more, he had to keep riding until he crossed the border into Mexico. Once there, he hoped he'd be far enough away to slowly forget Hannah and start life afresh. Perhaps he'd even find a woman he genuinely cared about, as he cared for Hannah. But he doubted it. Not just because most women wanted more from him than he was willing to give, but because he couldn't pinpoint why he'd been so drawn to Hannah. Sure, she was attractive, but so were many other women he'd known, and he'd never considered sharing his life with them. So, what was it? Could it be what she represented – a settled family life, someone to share his innermost feelings with, instead of keeping them all locked up inside him?

And if the latter were true, Drifter thought, why, after all his years of aimlessly drifting, should he suddenly care about such things? Hell, he'd never questioned himself before, so why now?

What had changed him?

He searched his mind, but couldn't think of any specific reason. It irked him. But right now, he thought, as he battled a jaw-cracking yawn, sleep was more important than worrying about the reason. So, resting his head on the sweet-smelling hay, he closed his eyes and was about to dismiss it from his mind, when a thought hit him like an avalanche.

He'd never been this old before!

CHAPTER
TWENTY-TWO

Dawn finally broke. The rising sun, resembling an orange wafer that appeared to be perched atop the distant mountains, greeted Drifter as he left the barn and headed for the water pump. As he washed up, the icy water chasing away any left-over sleep, the sky became flooded with brilliant reds and golds that gave the impression the heavens were on fire.

Shortly, as Drifter finished toweling himself off, he heard horses approaching in the distance. Quickly donning his shirt and knotting his kerchief around his neck, he buckled on his gun-belt, grabbed his Winchester and looked off into the sunlit desert. He was quickly joined by the two wolf dogs, which had also heard the horses coming. They came rushing out of the barn and crouched barking at the front gate.

The commotion brought a sleepy-eyed Drew busting out of the cabin. Shotgun in hand, he looked questioningly at Drifter, who stood cradling his rifle as he watched the riders drawing closer.

110

'Who is it?' Drew asked, squinting into the low sun. 'Can you make them out?'

'Yeah. It's Slade and the Iversons . . . with a bunch of Double-S riders.'

'You sure about that?'

'Yeah. Earlier, when the sun wasn't in my eyes, I recognized their horses.'

'Damn it!' Drew angrily kicked a pebble that went bouncing across the dirt. 'When am I going to realize that not everyone's word is Gospel?'

'I don't follow you.'

'Slade – he said his old man would give us till the end of the week to move out.'

'This ain't about you moving out,' Drifter said grimly.

'It ain't?'

'Uh-uh. This is strictly payback.'

'You've lost me.'

'It's simple, *compadre*. Yesterday I made a damned fool of Slade in front of his men, and I reckon that now he figures on returning the favor. What's more, he may have decided to include you and your family in his payback.'

'Serious?'

'Why not? Think about it. Every day Slade gets treated like dirt by his old man and doesn't have the guts to fight back . . .'

'So?'

'So, he sure as hell ain't about to take any crap from outsiders . . . specially from me, someone he's jealous of and truly hates.'

Drew frowned. 'Why would he be jealous of you?'

111

'It's a long story and one I buried years ago. But, simply put, his old man once favored me over his son . . . and Slade's never forgiven him or me for it.'

The revelation so surprised Drew that he couldn't think of anything to say.

'What really pisses me off,' Drifter continued, 'is that deep down I knew it would come to this. Knew it as plain as the sweat on my brow.' He paused and spat his disgust in the dirt. 'I mean, a fella don't need too many brains to know even a cowardly skunk like Slade can only take so much bullying before he retaliates.'

'Maybe so... but what else could you have done?'

'What I should've done – plugged the son-of-a-toad right there and then. What's more, in the past, I would've . . . without the slightest hesitation.'

'So, what stopped you?'

'I wish I knew, *compadre*. I've tried to figure it out, but all I can say is that in that split second before I pulled the trigger, I went soft and stupidly let him ride off.'

'I wouldn't call it stupid,' Drew said. 'I mean, could be you've just gotten tired of killing. Ever considered that?'

Drifter grunted in a way that could have meant anything.

'I'm no expert on the subject, Quint, but it seems to me that to keep gunning men down, no matter how much they deserve it, would gradually eat away at a fella – even a hardened gunfighter like you – and sooner or later would wear him down.'

'Maybe,' Drifter said, unconvinced. 'But if that's true, *compadre*, then all I can say is, I've picked one hell of a time to get a conscience!'

Drew wasn't listening. As if suddenly realizing just how close the approaching riders were, he hurried back into the cabin.

Drifter gave a troubled sigh and looked out across the sunburned desert. The riders were less than a quarter of a mile away now. Tension knotted his guts, and instinctively he hitched up his gun-belt and levered a round into the chamber of his Winchester. Then, shielding his eyes, he grimly watched as his enemies crossed a shallow, sun-scorched gully and came riding toward him.

CHAPTER
TWENTY-THREE

When Slade, the Iversons and the gunmen were within shooting distance of the cabin, they reined up, dismounted, and took cover behind one of the many sand dunes. Moments later, they crawled up the far side of the slope, peered over the top and aimed their rifles toward the cabin.

Drifter, who'd already ducked behind the buckboard, rested his Winchester atop the nearest rear wheel, curled his finger around the trigger and waited for Slade or one of the gunmen to show himself.

But before any of them appeared, Drew stuck his head out of the cabin door and yelled: 'Hey, Quint! Get in here! They can't shoot through these walls and maybe we can pick 'em off one by one.'

It made sense, but Drifter hesitated to comply. Retreat just wasn't his way. But as Slade and the gunmen opened fire and their bullets splintered the gate and fences around him, he knew it was only a matter of time before he was hit, maybe even killed –

and ducking low, he ran to the cabin.

Bullets chased him, kicking up the sand about his boots. One bullet ripped through his shirt sleeve, painfully searing his arm, forcing him to dive head-long through the open door.

Immediately, Drew slammed the door shut, helped Drifter up and then joined his wife who was firing out the window at the gunmen. Behind her, Lydon sat on the floor loading two old pistols. She looked up as Drifter took Hannah's place at the window and noticed the blood reddening his torn shirt sleeve.

'Y-you're arm, Mr Drifter – it's bleeding!'

'I'm OK,' he assured her. 'It's just a nick.'

'Here, let me look at that,' Hannah said, concerned.

Before Drifter could reply, bullets ricocheted off the window ledge, forcing everyone to hit the floor. As they did, the bullets smashed two Dresden porcelain china dinner plates that sat on the kitchen shelf.

'Wonderful!' Hannah grumbled. 'There goes the last of my mother's beautiful imported china!'

'Pa Drew never liked them dishes anyway,' Lydon began. 'He . . .'

Her words were drowned out as Drifter and Drew opened fire out the window. Their bullets kicked up sand along the crest of the dune, killing one gunman and wounding another, and forcing Slade and the Iversons to keep their heads down.

'I'm out!' Drew exclaimed, turning from the window. 'Here. . . .' He tossed his rifle to Hannah, who began reloading it. He then motioned to Lydon to hand him the pistols she was holding. 'Let me have those, young'un.'

Lydon handed her father the two old pistols and Drew rejoined Drifter at the window.

'We've got to find a way to root them out of there,' Drifter said. 'Otherwise, they're going to keep us holed up in here while they burn us out.'

Drew nodded. At the same time, he fired several rounds at Mace Iverson, who was crawling between some rocks toward a dune that was closer to the cabin. Drew's bullets ricocheted off the rocks, causing flying chips to spatter over Mace. Alarmed, he scrambled back behind the dune.

'There is one way we might drive them out into the open,' Drew said. 'Though I wouldn't recommend it – not if a fella wants to see the sun come up tomorrow.'

'Tell me anyway,' Drifter said. He snapped off two quick shots, and a gunman who'd stuck his head over the top of the dune yelped and disappeared.

'Well, truth is, a while back I started to turn our cellar into a storm shelter. I never finished it, because the walls, being sand, kept caving in before I could shore them up. Also, by then I'd run out of lumber. And to make matters worse, the rains were extra heavy that year and. . . .'

Drifter cut him off. 'Does it have an exit?'

'Sure. One of those bolted-down tornado doors behind the cabin. 'Course by now I'm sure it's blocked off by falling sand.'

'Only one way to find out,' Drifter said. Turning to Hannah, he added: 'I need you to help Drew keep them pinned down for a few minutes – you know, just long enough so I can sneak out of the cellar. You OK with that?'

'Of course,' she said. 'But, like my husband said, I'm sure the cellar's full of sand now.'

Drifter shrugged. 'If it is, then we'll just have to figure out something else.' He turned back to Drew, saying: 'Let's go, *amigo*!'

'Wait!' Lydon said anxiously. 'W-what if you get killed? What're we supposed to do then?'

'Lydon, for heaven's sake!' exclaimed her mother.

'It's OK,' Drifter said. He bent beside Lydon. 'That's a fair question, missy, and with all honesty all I can say is, I'm counting on you to help keep me safe.'

'M-me?'

'Sure.'

'How?'

'Keep reloading your folks' guns. That way, they can pin down Stadtlander's men long enough for me to make a break for it.' He fondly tousled her hair, then joined Drew, who'd already lifted a trapdoor in the floor, which led to the cellar.

Lydon chewed her lip and stared anxiously after Drifter. Then controlling her fear, she bravely got up and took a box of shells to her mother, who was firing out the window.

Drew, eager to join Hannah, held Drifter's rifle while handing him a lighted kerosene lamp. 'Here, you'll need this.'

'Thanks.' Drifter, lamp held before him, started down the steps. When he reached the bottom, he reached back up to Drew, who gave him the Winchester.

'Good luck, partner.'

'*Gracias, compadre.*' Drifter, stooping over so that his head didn't hit the low ceiling, squeezed between the piles of sand that in places blocked his way to the steps leading up to the exit door.

CHAPTER
TWENTY-FOUR

When Drifter finally reached the steps, he paused and held up the lamp. Its light revealed that the steps were half buried by fallen sand. He quickly scooped away enough of it to make room for himself, and then started climbing up to the exit.

As he climbed, he could hear muffled rifle fire outside. Using the sound to hide any noise he made, he forced open the rusted clasp fastening the hinged tornado door. It took a few moments to loosen it. But once he had succeeded, he then blew out the lamp, waited until his eyes adjusted to the dark, and inched open the door.

The desert echoed with incessant rifle fire. Drifter left the lamp on the top step and slowly raised the door enough so that he could slide out under it. The bright sunlight made him squint. Remaining on his hands and knees, he crawled to a nearby clump of creosote bushes. The hot sand burned his palms, but he finally reached the flowering evergreen bushes and took cover there.

For once fate was on Drifter's side. The cabin not only hid him from Slade and the gunmen, but the corner nearest Drifter was close to the corrals. He made it there quickly. Then, making sure his Winchester was fully loaded, he ducked low and ran to the nearest corral. He made the fence unseen and flopped down on his belly.

The rifle fire from the cabin window was now intermittent and Drifter guessed that the Albrights were running low on ammo.

Slade, the Iverson brothers and the remaining gunmen must have guessed the same thing because as Drifter watched between the bars of the corral fence, all of them left the protection of the sand dune. Then, once in the open, they scattered to make themselves harder targets, many of them ducking behind the rocky outcrops and clumps of giant cacti that offered them cover between the dune and the cabin.

As Drifter grimly watched Slade and his gunmen advancing toward the cabin, he knew it was up to him to stop them from killing the Albrights. And no matter the personal risk, he had to do it *now!*

Rifle in hand, he slid under the bottom bar of the corral fence and circled around behind the gunmen. There, he took cover behind another creosote bush. Heart thudding and sweat pouring off his face, he peered between the leaves and caught a glimpse of the Iversons. They were crouched behind some rocks, well within rifle range. But unfortunately, he couldn't see enough of either brother to guarantee killing or even wounding them. Worse, he knew that once he opened fire, he'd not only give away his position to Slade and the gunmen, but the Iversons would then crawl farther behind the rocks, giving him no target.

Frustrated, Drifter suddenly noticed a large cone-shaped mound within a few feet of the rocks hiding the Iversons. Realizing what it was, he smiled to himself. He then carefully aimed at the upper part of the mound and fired several times.

His bullets chopped off the top of the cone. He was too far away to see exactly what havoc he'd caused, but within minutes Drifter heard the Iversons cursing and yelping in pain. Moments later, the two brothers burst out from behind the rocks. After a few steps, they began hopping around, frantically slapping at the mass of fire ants angrily swarming up their legs.

Drifter took quick aim at Cody, who was closest, and squeezed the trigger.

Cody gasped, clutched his belly, stumbled forward, and collapsed.

Drifter quickly fired again, his second shot punching a hole in Mace's chest. Eyes wide with shock, Mace briefly staggered forward and then dropped to his knees and fell, face down, on top of the ant hill.

As Drifter watched, a seething red blanket of fire ants swarmed over Mace's corpse.

Nearby, Slade and the gunmen, realizing they were being attacked from two sides, quickly retreated and took cover behind the same sand dune where they'd left their horses. They didn't offer much of a target, but Drifter helped them on their way with a few shots, his bullets whining about their ears like angry hornets.

Finally, magazine now empty, he quickly reloaded.

As he did, he recognized one of the last gunmen to take cover. He only caught a glimpse of the man's face and for a moment, Drifter couldn't place him. And then it hit him: it was Hal Fermin – the same gaunt, thin-faced Hal Fermin that Drifter had seen earlier watching him from the saloon. It then dawned on him that Fermin must be responsible for bringing Slade and the gunmen to the Albrights' cabin in the hope of killing Drifter and the Albrights at the same time. Word of their death would then spread to the other farmers and settlers, warning them to abandon their homesteads and leave the valley or face the Albrights' fate. Once they were gone, Slade could then win his father's affection by triumphantly explaining that now, thanks to him, the entire range belonged to the Stadtlanders!

The thought enraged Drifter, and he silently vowed to put an end to Stadtlander's greedy plans, once and for all. But in order to do that, he knew he'd have to set aside his own goal – which was to permanently hang up his guns. Still, he didn't hesitate. Important as that was to him, it would have to wait. Unless, of course, he selfishly abandoned Drew and his family and rode off. Which he couldn't do. Not and still live with himself. So he decided to end the distasteful task ahead of him as fast as possible.

Making sure that none of the gunmen were looking his way, he crawled under the fence and across the corral to the gate. Here, partially protected by the nearest post, he stood up, brushed the hot sand from his blistered palms, rested his rifle atop the fence and aimed at the nearest gunman. Then, timing his shot so that it blended in with the rifle fire of the other gunmen, Drifter squeezed the trigger.

The Winchester bucked against his shoulder. An instant later the gunman dropped his rifle, slumped over and slowly crumpled to the dirt.

Drifter didn't see the man die. He'd already slid his rifle barrel along the top of the fence, lined up his next target and fired. The crash of his rifle was again hidden by all the gunfire. The bullet struck the gunman at the base of his skull. His head snapped back, blood spurting from under the brim of his hat. Then, as if life was repeating itself, he slumped to the ground.

Drifter snapped off a third shot. His aim was true – but this time the gunman cried out before he died, and his scream was heard by Slade and the other gunmen. As one, they stopped firing and quickly turned toward the victim, in time to see him collapse. They also saw Drifter as he ducked behind the gatepost, and immediately opened fire at him.

Their bullets splintered the bars of the fence dangerously close to Drifter's head, forcing him to flop to the ground and start crawling back to the barn.

Even though partly protected by the fence, he never would have made it but for Drew's help. Wondering why Slade and the gunmen had stopped firing at the cabin, Drew cautiously poked his head out the window and saw what was happening in the corral. He immediately told Hannah, and together they started shooting the last of their bullets at the gunmen.

Their accuracy kept Slade and his men pinned

down long enough for Drifter to scramble under the fence and run safely back behind the cabin. There, as he went to reload, he realized that he, too, was running low on ammo. But though he only had three rounds left, he wasn't worried since he always kept a spare box of 45-70 shells for his Winchester in his saddlebag. But he needed them quickly. And peering around the corner of the cabin, he made sure Slade and the gunmen were still pinned down, and then bolted for the barn.

CHAPTER TWENTY-FIVE

Once safely in the barn, Drifter hurried to his saddle that hung over the stall holding his horse. Opening his saddlebag, he grabbed the box of shells and ran back outside. There, protected by the cabin, he paused and listened for a moment. He could hear the gunmen firing, but could not hear return fire from in the cabin. Figuring that Drew had finally run out of ammo, Drifter went to the storm shelter.

Raising the tornado door, he climbed inside and fumbled around until he found the kerosene lamp he'd left on the top step. Digging out one of the loose matches he always kept in his shirt pocket, he struck it against his thumbnail. A tiny flame flared, flickered and almost went out. Drifter quickly shielded it with his free hand. And once the flame grew steady, he picked up the lamp, removed the glass chimney and lit the wick. Then holding the lamp before him, he descended the steps and made his way through the sand piles to the opposite steps. The cellar door was still open. Drifter ducked inside and entered the cabin. Here he found Drew, Hannah and Lydon piling all the furniture against the front door.

Relieved to see him, they stopped what they were doing and anxiously gathered about him. Drew started to explain that they had run out of ammunition, but Drifter cut him off, saying: 'Hang on a moment!'

'Why? What's wrong?' Drew asked.

'Move everything away from the door!'

'B-but what about those men out. . . ?'

Drifter cut Drew off. 'I don't have time to explain, *compadre*. But I got an idea. Trust me,' he insisted when they stared doubtfully at him. 'This is the only way any of us are going to get out of here alive!'

Giving them no time to argue, he set the lamp down and started moving the furniture.

Drew hesitated for another moment, and then turned to his wife and daughter. 'Do as he says,' he ordered. 'Now!' He then joined Drifter, and together they dragged the heavy dinner table aside.

Hannah and Lydon quickly joined in.

'OK,' Drifter said, when all the furniture was moved. 'Here's what I want you to do.' Picking up Drew's empty rifle, he thrust it into Hannah's hands and opened the door.

'Y-you want me to go out there?' she said, surprised. 'Yeah.'

'No!' Drew exclaimed. 'She can't, Quint! I won't let her! My God, man, those devils out there will gun her down as fast as they can pull the trigger.'

'Not until they've had their fun with her,' Drifter

126

said grimly.

Hannah looked horrified. 'You want them to . . . to violate me?

'I want them to *think* they're going to,' Drifter corrected. 'In fact, I'm counting on it.'

Hannah still hesitated.

'Please,' Drifted insisted. 'Do as I say. Go on, get out there! You too,' he added to Drew and Lydon. 'And remember, all of you, if they ask about me, tell them that I'm all shot up and you're surrendering!'

CHAPTER TWENTY-SIX

From their vantage point behind the rocks Slade and the remaining gunmen stopped shooting as they saw the Albrights step out of the cabin, throw down their guns and raise their hands in surrender.

'Don't shoot!' Drew yelled. 'We're all out of ammo!'

Slade eyed him suspiciously. 'What about Drifter?' he demanded.

'He's in the barn,' Drew lied. 'Gut shot!'

'He going to make it?'

'Not unless we get him to town real fast. And even then, chances are he'll bleed out before the doctor can save him.'

'How do I know you ain't lying?' Slade persisted.

'You don't,' Drew admitted. 'But ask yourself this: would you lie in my position – out of ammo and with your wife and daughter standing beside you?'

'I reckon not.' Slade stepped out from behind the rocks, gun in hand, and confronted the Albrights. 'So, the question now is, what to do with you: shoot you, or string you up to the nearest tree.'

'Quit trying to throw a scare into us,' Drew said. 'Not even you would hang a woman or a child.'

'Why not? Who's to stop me?' Slade grinned at his men. 'Right, boys?'

The men laughed and some of them made crude sexual gestures to Hannah.

'Please, Slade,' Drew pleaded. 'I'm begging you. Don't shoot us. Just give us time to load our things on to the wagon and we'll go.'

'Go?' Slade questioned. 'Go, where?'

'Arizona,' Hannah said, thinking on her feet.

Slade frowned at her, puzzled. ''Mean, you're leaving for good?'

'That is what your father wants, isn't it?' she said. 'Us gone, so he can graze his cattle on our land?'

'Sure . . .'

'Then, tell him he's got his wish.'

'Be glad to,' Slade said. 'But what about me, woman?' He grinned lecherously at her. 'Pa ain't the only Stadtlander who's got needs. What's in it for me if I let you go?'

Drew started to respond. But quickly Hannah raised her hand, silencing him, then said to Slade: 'That depends.'

'On what?'

'What you want.'

'That's easy,' he leered. 'You!'

'Go to hell,' Drew began angrily.

Hannah cut him off. 'No, no, honey, it's his right. Like he says. If he lets us live, he deserves to get something in return.'

'Maybe. But that don't include you . . .'

'It does if you don't want me to kill all three of you!' Slade threatened.

Drew started to reply, but Hannah, seeing the rage in his eyes and realizing he must have forgotten Drifter's plan, again cut him off.

'Please,' she said, grasping his hand, 'don't interfere, honey. It's our lives we're talking about. Mine, yours and Lydon's!'

'Exactly! Which is why I . . .'

'Please, Drew,' she begged, 'just do as I ask!' She hugged him fondly, at the same time whispering so that only he could hear: 'Trust . . . Drifter . . .' She then stepped back and beckoned to Slade, 'C'mon . . .' and entered the cabin.

Slade sneered at Drew. 'Count yourself lucky, sodbuster! Your woman just saved your miserable life!' Signaling to the gunmen to keep Drew and Lydon covered, he ducked into the cabin.

Lydon fearfully grabbed Drew's hand. 'Stop him, Pa!' she begged. 'He's going to hurt Momma. . . .'

'Hush, sweetheart . . .' Drew pulled her close and kissed the top of the head. 'Everything's going to be all right. I promise.'

In the cabin, Hannah stood facing Slade as he paused with his back to the door and looked suspiciously about him. 'You ain't fooling me, Quint,' he said loudly. 'I know you're in here. . . .'

'Weren't you listening earlier?' Hannah said. 'Drifter's in the barn. Hurt.'

Slade ignored her. Cocking his six-gun, he first looked behind the broken-legged table and then cautiously inched toward the overturned couch.

'Damn you, woman!' he exclaimed when he saw the soles of Drifter's boots poking out from one end. 'I'm going to make you sorry for lying to me . . .' He broke off, startled, as Drifter, bare-footed, stepped out from behind the still-open door and pressed his Winchester against Slade's neck.

'Still making threats you can't keep, eh, sonny?' Drifter said mockingly.

Slade panicked. 'W-wait. . . !' he exclaimed, raising his hands. 'I wasn't going to hurt her, Quint, I swear.'

Drifter grunted disgustedly. 'You know, I underestimated you, Slade. I had you pegged as just a gutless coward, but it turns out you're a no-good chicken-livered liar as well!'

Slade went white with rage but was too scared to say anything.

Drifter stepped in front of him and thumbed back the hammer of his rifle. 'So how do you want it, sonny? In the belly or 'tween the eyes?'

Slade stumbled back, fearfully, and dropped to his knees. 'P-please,' he begged, 'I'll do anything you want – *anything* – but please, please, don't shoot me.'

Drifter stared at him, death in his gray eyes, just itching to pull the trigger.

'No, no, Quint!' Hannah quickly grabbed his arm. 'It's all right. There's no need to kill him. He's learned his lesson. Let him go.'

Drifter looked at her in disbelief. 'Let him go?'

'Yes.'

'But, why?'

'Because I don't want to be responsible for anyone's death. Not even his.'

'You ain't responsible, Hannah. I'm the one pulling the trigger.'

'It's the same thing.' She paused, saw the hate in his eyes, then said: 'Please, Quint ... if I mean anything to you, you won't kill him.'

Drifter argued briefly with himself, and then grudgingly relented. 'You do realize, Hannah, if I let him and these other weasels go, it won't end here? Old Man Stadtlander will never stop trying to steal your land for his cattle.'

'He won't have to steal it, Quint. He can have it, free.'

'Meaning?'

'Last night, Drew and I decided that our lives – and Lydon's life – are worth far more than this miserable little piece of dirt. So we're going to pack up and move.'

'To where?' Drifter said, dreading her answer.

'We're not exactly sure yet. But my father owns parcels of land throughout the southwest, and I know he'd be only too delighted to give us as many acres as we want – just so long as it meant I was going to live near him.' She turned to Slade, adding: 'Tell that to your father. Make him understand that all Drew and I need is enough time to gather up our things and move out. Then the land's his. All right?'

'S-sure,' Slade said, relieved. 'I'll tell Pa. Got my word on it, ma'am.' To Drifter, he added: 'OK if I get up, mister?'

'First, give me your iron.'

Then as Slade handed over his six-gun:

'OK, on your feet!' Drifter tucked Slade's gun in his

belt and wagged his Winchester at him, indicating he could get up. Then, when Slade was on his feet, Drifter kicked open the door and followed him out into the bright hot sunlight.

CHAPTER
TWENTY-SEVEN

Outside, Drifter handed Slade his six-gun. 'Leather it!'

Slade obeyed.

Behind him, the mounted gunmen looked on curiously.

Drifter unhooked the tiny safety strap on his holster and faced Slade. 'You got two choices, sonny. Jerk that iron, or go to jail. What's it going to be?'

Trapped, Slade licked his lips uneasily. He desperately wanted to kill Drifter but didn't have the guts to draw. But he didn't want to go to jail, either. What made it worse, his father wasn't there to advise him or bail him out of trouble. This was one decision he'd have to make on his own. But unfortunately he realized that meant he'd also be responsible for the consequences, no matter what they turned out to be.

The thought panicked Slade. And unable to handle the pressure alone, he turned to his gunmen, his expression begging them for help.

His cowardice brought scorn to their grim faces. At one time or another, they had all taken abuse from

Slade, and to see him being humiliated this way was kind of satisfying. At the same time, he *was* their boss and they wanted him to be man enough to stand up to Drifter. Instead, he had crumpled! Disgusted by his yellow streak, they shifted uncomfortably in their saddles and finally looked away.

'Fair enough,' Drifter said, tired of waiting for Slade to decide. 'Drop your gun-belt, sonny, and give me your rifle. I'm taking you into town and handing you over to Sheriff Forbes. As for you men,' he added to the gunmen, 'you'd better ride back to the Double-S and tell Stadtlander that his son is sitting in jail!'

As one, the gunmen looked at Slade for orders. Then, when he wouldn't meet their eyes, they turned their horses around and rode away.

At that moment, Lydon saw a large yellow-and-black butterfly flit past. Despite the drama going on around her, she gave a tiny gasp of joy and pointed it out to her mother. 'Look, look, Momma, a swallowtail!'

Drifter, momentarily distracted, looked toward the butterfly.

It was all Slade needed. He went for his gun.

'Quint!' Drew yelled.

He needn't have worried. Drifter, ever aware of Slade's treachery, was already reaching for his Colt.

He cleared leather first and fired from the hip.

Slade staggered back, his life ebbing from the hole in his heart, and after a few wobbly steps sank to the ground.

Drifter moved close and cautiously prodded the corpse with the toe of his boot.

It didn't move.

Satisfied that Slade was dead, Drifter faced the Albrights. Their somber, tight-lipped expressions jarred him. The look in their eyes told him they had seen death before, but never this close up or in the brutally dispassionate way that Drifter had just dealt it out.

Hannah looked at Drifter as if seeing him not only for the first time, but for what he truly was: an aging, hardened gunfighter who brought death with him wherever he went.

Stung by their silent condemnation of him, Drifter hid his feelings and, ever taciturn, said only: 'Listen to me. All of you. Despite what you may think, I ain't trying to get you involved in this war. That's the last thing I'd ever do. But I would ask you this: if it ever came down to it and the law asked you to tell what you saw, remember – Slade drew first.'

For a moment neither Drew, Hannah nor Lydon said anything.

Then Drew, speaking for all of them, started to respond. But his throat had gone dry and he struggled to find his voice. He licked his lips, swallowed hard, and when he finally managed to speak, he sounded as if he were talking to a stranger. 'S-sure, Quint. Sure. We won't forget . . . that's a promise.'

'Fair enough,' Drifter said, adding: 'I'll be taking the body back to his father now.'

Lydon, silent up till now, couldn't restrain herself any longer. 'No, no, you mustn't!' she cried. 'Mr Stadtlander, he'll kill you!'

Drifter smiled and fondly ruffled her hair. 'Don't worry, young'un. I don't intend to give him the chance.'

136

'B-but . . .'

Hannah pulled her close, saying 'Hush, child . . .' and they remained cuddled together, watching as Drifter and Drew draped Slade's corpse over the back of his horse.

Then Drifter mounted the sorrel, took the reins of Slade's horse from Drew, and with a throwaway salute, rode off.

Lydon watched them ride away. Then turning to her father, she said tearfully: 'Pa, do you reckon we'll ever see Mr Drifter again?'

'Of course,' Drew lied. 'Sooner or later he'll drift by again . . .' As he spoke, he looked at Hannah and thought: *Only we won't be here any longer. And maybe that's just as well.*

CHAPTER
TWENTY-EIGHT

Stillman J. Stadtlander stood on the front porch of his large, impressive ranch-house, looking on as two of his gunmen lifted Slade's corpse off his horse. Tears ran down the rancher's tanned leathery cheeks and his chest heaved with sobs. . . .

Drifter, watching him from beside the sorrel, realized for the first time that despite Stadtlander's belligerent, chest-thumping and boastful talk of vengeance, he had feelings like any other man. It was a Stadtlander that Drifter had never known or even believed existed, and he had a hard time hiding his surprise.

'Where do you want us to put him, boss?' one of the gunmen asked Stadtlander.

'In his room on . . .' Tears choked off the rancher's voice. He had to take several deep breaths before he could continue. 'And when you lay him on his bed, handle him gently, or by God I'll make you both sorry you were ever born!'

'Y-yes, boss.'

'And when you're done, one of you ride into town and fetch the undertaker.'

'Sure thing, boss.'

Stadtlander waited until the two gunmen had carried Slade's corpse into the house, then he descended the porch steps and angrily confronted Drifter.

'I reckon you think you've won, don't you?'

Drifter shrugged and remained silent.

'Well, think again, Longley!' Stadtlander raged through his tears. 'Because this'll never be over. Not so long as I've got a single breath in my body! No matter where you go or how long it takes me, sooner or later I'll find you, damn it, and bring you down!'

'Why wait?' Drifter said quietly. 'What's wrong with now? I'm here, Stillman, standing right in front of you. I mean, you ain't likely to ever get a better chance than this.'

'You'd like that, wouldn't you?' Stadtlander sneered. 'Then you could brag to the world how you murdered me and my son on the same day!'

'I didn't "murder" nobody!'

'Says you!'

'Not just me. Ask your men. They were there. They saw Slade throw down on me. All I done was what any man would do – protect myself.'

'Liar!'

Drifter tensed, and the blood seemed to drain from his hawkish face. 'You ain't yourself right now,' he said grimly, 'so I'll let that ride. But I warn you, Stillman, if you ever call me a liar again, you better be packing iron.'

'Save your threats!' Stadtlander snarled. 'They don't frighten me!' He fisted the tears from his eyes before adding: 'They ain't going to make me change my mind, either. I knew my son, better than anybody. And much as I loved him, I never had any delusions about him. He was a gutless coward, through and through. Which is why I know you're lying. Slade would've run off like a scared jack rabbit before he'd ever slap leather with you!'

'Not if my back was turned.'

It was the ultimate insult and Stadtlander cringed. What made it even worse, he didn't doubt that Drifter was telling the truth . . . and that only made him angrier.

'You're wasting your breath!' he hissed. 'Nothing you can say will ever convince me that you didn't murder my boy . . . *or* stop me from one day killing you! Now, get the hell off my ranch!'

Drifter knew it was useless to argue. He'd known Stadtlander for many years and during that time had never met a more pig-headed man. So, rather than add to his frustration, Drifter moved sideways to his horse and grasped the reins. Then, still facing Stadtlander, eyes locked on the enraged rancher, he stepped into the stirrup, grabbed the pommel and pulled himself up into the saddle. Drifter then slowly backed up the sorrel, one hand on his pistol, ready to shoot Stadtlander or any of the gunmen who attempted to draw.

None did.

Drifter continued to back up until he was satisfied that no one was going to try to kill him, then he swung the sorrel around and rode off.

CHAPTER TWENTY-NINE

Though not unduly alarmed by Stadtlander's threat, Drifter was wise enough to know that from now on he had another reason to be wary of anyone who got within gunshot of him. Keeping that in mind, he figured that the best way to minimize the potential danger was to put as many miles between himself and Stadtlander's gunmen as fast as possible. Jamming his hat firmly on his head, he spurred the sorrel into a steady, loping gallop and rode back to town.

He intended to ride on through Santa Rosa without stopping and then continue northward along the near-desolate Pacific coastline until he felt safe enough to start drifting again. But when he reached town, it was already growing dark and he was famished. Knowing the sorrel was just as hungry, Drifter left the weary horse at the livery stable for Lars to feed, crossed the street and entered the Copper Palace.

He'd planned on enjoying a thick burnt steak and fried potatoes with a beer or two to quench his thirst.

But as he elbowed his way up to the bar, word from the people who'd seen him ride into town had spread ahead of him and he was surrounded by grateful citizens. They insisted on buying his dinner and drinks, and then, on seeing how trail weary he was, ignored his protests and paid for a hotel room.

That wasn't all. Rumors that Stadtlander intended to kill Drifter had somehow preceded him, and several concerned men had armed themselves and posted lookouts behind barriers at each end of town, just in case the gunmen showed up.

Drifter, overwhelmed by their generosity, wolfed down his meal, even polishing off a wedge of hot apple pie and ice cream. Then, his belly threatening to burst, he plodded upstairs to his room and wearily fell into bed.

Roosters woke him the following dawn. Splashing cold water on his face, he dressed, went downstairs, crossed the street and entered the livery stable. There, Lars was already up and enjoying his coffee. He poured Drifter a cup and grimly explained that he had bad news: a cowhand who'd once run beef out at the Double-S had stopped by last night to have his horse reshod. While he waited for Lars to finish shoeing, he'd mentioned that Stadtlander was hiring more gunmen.

Drifter looked surprised. 'He must think I'm more of a problem than I thought.'

'It ain't just you,' Lars said. 'The no-good weasel also intends to burn down Santa Rosa in revenge for Slade's death. In fact,' he added, 'there's a meeting going on in the Copper Palace as we speak.'

143

'Why ain't you there?'

'Now that I've given you your coffee, I'd intend to be.'

'Count me in.'

'I was hoping you'd say that.'

Drifter looked offended. 'Mean, you weren't sure I'd throw in with you?'

Lars shrugged. 'I ain't sure about nothing these days.'

'Thanks.'

'No need to get snarky, Quint. You ain't exactly known to be civic-minded . . . or for settling down.'

Drifter, pinned by the truth, gulped down his coffee. Then he and Lars left the stable and crossed the street to the saloon.

CHAPTER THIRTY

The meeting was breaking up when Drifter and Lars entered the saloon, and most of the men were leaving to defend the barricades at each end of town. Lars stopped one of the farmers he knew and asked him how the vote went.

'Without a hitch,' he replied. 'To a man, we all decided that we'd had enough of Stadtlander's bullying, and agreed that from now on we'd fight him, tooth and nail, and hope that sooner or later he realizes that trying to steal our land is too costly, and grazes his beef elsewhere!' He paused, spat chaw juice into a nearby spittoon, then added: 'It'd be a gift from heaven if he did, but, like I told the others, knowing Old Man Stadtlander like we do, I wouldn't bet my farm on it.' He walked off before Lars could question him further.

'Pitchforks against six-guns,' Drifter growled. 'Sure, that works!'

'Don't underestimate them,' Lars said. 'When you've fought the land all your life, like Zeb and the other farmers have, fighting a bunch of hired gunnies don't seem so daunting.'

'Be sure to write that on their tombstones,' Drifter said. 'It'll make a nice epitaph!'

'Cut it out,' Lars grumbled. 'These are fine, decent folks we're talking about.'

'Which is *exactly* why you got to stop them from becoming martyrs!'

'How? You heard Zeb. They're all riled up and itching for a fight.'

'Which they'll end up regretting, trust me.'

'I do. But you're missing the point. I ain't the one who needs convincing.'

'No, but these men will listen to you.'

'So?'

'So, talk to them. Make them understand that it's easy to talk a fight, but a whole different story to actually *fight* one.'

'They already know that. But at this stage, what else can they do?'

'Caution's the way.'

'There was a time, bucko, when you could've sold them on that. Not now. Like Zeb just said, none of the farmers hereabouts is of a mind to be pushed around any more. Same with the townsfolk. They've all decided to make a stand.'

'Brave talk.'

'Not brave, Quint. Backs-against-the-wall talk!'

'Don't matter. It's still talk. And talk won't stop bullets. A lot of these men are going to end up dead.'

'If you truly believe that,' Lars said, watching the grim-faced farmers and townspeople marching out the door, 'then do something about it.'

146

'Me? What the hell have I got to do with it?'

'Plenty! You've been the example, Quint. You stood up to Stadtlander and showed these men that they can do likewise.'

'Oh-h no,' Drifter said, 'You ain't pinning this on *me, compadre.*'

'Well, I'm right sorry to hear that. 'Cause, like it or not, you started it.'

'I don't see it that way.'

'Then "see" this: when all a man's got is his kinfolk, fields to plow, a store to run and hopefully a roof over his head, they can be powerful persuaders when it comes to fighting to keep them. I don't expect you to understand that, bucko, you being an orphan and always on the drift. But take it from me, when most folks think their home is in jeopardy, they'll find the backbone to protect it.'

'Easy to say that now,' Drifter said. 'But not when bullets are flying and loved ones are dying.'

Lars gave an exasperated snort and wagged his finger in Drifter's face. 'Make no mistake, bucko! No one's taking this lightly, including yours truly. We all know there's going to be plenty of blood spilled today. But we also know that not all of it's going to be spilled on our side of the barricades. And our hope is that when Stadtlander sees we ain't folding, and realizes he can't bully us no more, being the coward that he is, he'll think twice before he tries it again.' Lars paused as a group of farmers beckoned to him. Then excusing himself, he hurried over to join them.

Alone, Drifter chewed thoughtfully on Lars' words, and realized how well the old stableman had him

147

pegged. He'd never known a real home. Hell, he couldn't even remember his parents. As for the orphanage, his only childhood memories were cruelly painful and full of harsh loneliness. He'd put up with it because he had nowhere else to go. But finally, on reaching his teens, he grew so sick of all the beatings and always being hungry, he rebelled. And one night, when everyone was asleep, he broke out, stole the preacher's horse and rode it until it collapsed from exhaustion.

By then it was daylight and he'd reached the out-skirts of a small town. Half-starved, he'd sneaked around, eating whatever he could find in garbage bins and gutters. Then, chased off by the sheriff, he'd hidden among the luggage atop a stagecoach that took him to the next town. There he'd jumped off, unseen, and broken into a gun store. Not knowing anything about guns, he'd stolen the first pistol he saw: a long-barreled, single-shot Navy Colt that felt clumsy in his hands. But determined to get skillful with it, he kept practising and practising until finally, months later, he became so proficient that he used it to rob banks and stores in one sleepy little town after another. But though the law never caught him, life on the run as a wanted outlaw had eventually gotten old, and once Drifter became an adult, he'd buried his name and the past and started drifting from one ranch to another.

Now, thinking about those years, Drifter realized that drifting was all he'd ever known. He'd never gotten married and never owned a spread of his own. So how the devil could he be expected to care about something he knew nothing about, much less fight for it?

Then it dawned on him that the closest thing he'd ever had to a home was Santa Rosa. Year after year, no matter where he went or how long he was gone, just like a homing pigeon, he always found himself back here. What's more, thanks to friends like Lars, he felt comfortable here. Even safe. Well, as safe as anyone in his profession could ever feel.

And now, Stadtlander and his hired gunnies intended to burn Santa Rosa down and leave nothing for Drifter to remember but smoldering ashes!

Enraged by the idea, he promised himself that he'd find some way to force Stadtlander to permanently back off – even if it meant killing him! And when Lars rejoined him, Drifter, with renewed optimism, grasped the old stableman's arm and steered him to the door, saying: 'Let's have that coffee, *compadre*. And then we'll figure out the best way to protect this town of ours.'

CHAPTER
THIRTY-ONE

It was later that same day that Zane Crawley, one of two lookouts perched atop the sand dunes at the north end of town, saw horsemen riding across the sunbaked desert toward him. Even from a distance he could see they were led by Stadtlander and Clay Hudson, and quickly turning to the men and women crouched behind the makeshift barrier below him, he pumped his rifle above his head three times.

Seeing the signal, Drifter, Lars and the hardened settlers grimly prepared to repel their attackers. Lars, knowing they'd need every man available, fired a shot in the air, alerting the farmers guarding the south end of town. They responded by climbing on to their wagons and riding up Front Street to join their comrades.

They didn't have long to wait. Even as dusk approached, Stadtlander and his gunmen came riding toward them. But instead of attacking the town, as everyone expected, they reined up and took cover behind one of the nearby dunes.

'What the devil's he up to?' Lars asked Drifter. 'Is he waiting for darkness?'

Before Drifter could reply, Stadtlander and Clay Hudson rode out from behind the dune. Stadtlander was holding a rifle with a white rag tied to the barrel, and when he was within earshot of the barrier, he reined up and signaled that he wanted to talk.

'Hold your fire, men,' Lars yelled. 'Let's hear what he's got to say.'

'No matter *what* he says,' Drifter warned, 'don't trust him!'

'I won't,' Lars said. 'But we got nothing to lose by listening to him.'

Drifter's half-hearted shrug suggested he didn't agree. But all he said was: 'It's your call, *compadre*. But don't be surprised if one of his men takes a shot at you.'

It was a sobering thought. But Lars decided to trust his instincts. Rising, he poked his head above the barrier and faced Stadtlander, saying: 'Go ahead, Stillman. Speak your piece.'

'I intend to,' the belligerent rancher replied. 'What's more, you all better listen, 'cause I've reached the end of my patience.'

'Quit being a blowhard,' Drifter growled. 'Get to the point!'

'My point is,' Stadtlander said, 'I'm giving all you sodbusters a choice: turn your farms over to me and get out of the valley, or face the consequences!'

'Which are?' Lars demanded.

'Be driven off by my men . . . and none too gently, neither!'

'That works both ways,' warned an elderly farmer. 'Your gunmen better get ready for one hell of a fight, 'cause I promise you, Stadtlander, none of us is going to give up our land while we're still breathing!'

'Amen,' agreed another farmer. ''Tween Indians and Comancheros, we've been fighting for our farms *and* our lives ever since we settled here. So your threats ain't nothing new!'

'Comancheros murdered my folks,' a third farmer said bitterly. 'Strung 'em up in front of me and my sister when we was just little shavers. Can remember it as if it was yesterday. All of 'em drunk on mescal, staggering about, laughing, setting fire to everything, shooting our livestock, even the chickens, leaving us nothing to eat, and then riding off 'fore the smoke brought our neighbors a-running.' He paused, eaten up by his gut-wrenching memories, then glaring defiantly at Stadtlander, and added: 'But me and my sis are still here, raising families, battling droughts, sandstorms, dying crops, you name it. What's more, despite your constant bullying, we're going to *keep* on being here long after you're dead!'

Stirred by his words, all the other farmers started cheering.

'Suit yourselves,' Stadtlander said. 'But I promise you, leave this valley you will, even if it's feet up! The same goes for the rest of you folks,' he warned the townspeople. 'You're all going to pay for the death of my son! I'm going to burn Santa Rosa to ground, and anyone who tries to stop me or my men, will be gunned down! The choice is yours!'

'That ain't no choice,' Lars said, 'it's an ultimatum!'

Angry murmurs of agreement arose from the armed men and the women lined along the barricade.

'Call it what you like,' Stadtlander sneered, 'it makes no difference to me. Only thing I care about is your answer!' He paused to let his words sink in, then said:

'So, what's it going to be – leave, or eat lead?'

There was a hushed silence.

Then, Drifter stepped out from behind the barrier and confronted Stadtlander.

'Stillman,' he said softly, 'I don't have a dog in this fight. My quarrel's strictly with you. And I'm going to get great satisfaction out of knowing that thanks to me, after today you won't be alive to see *anyone* driven off their land!'

Stadtlander licked his lips uneasily. Then with false bravado, he tried to laugh off Drifter's threat. 'We'll see about that, Longley,' he said, and nodded at Clay.

It was the signal that the immaculately dressed little gunman had been waiting for. He smiled cruelly and dismounted. He then confronted Drifter, his gray-gloved hands hovering above his two pearl-handled pistols. 'Ready to die, gunny?'

Drifter grinned tauntingly at him. 'Always – *Shorty!*'

Clay lost his smile. His ice-blue eyes narrowed in a cold fury. He tensed, as if gathering all his energy, and then reached for his guns.

He was fast – even faster than everyone looking on had expected.

Drifter was faster.

Barely.

He drew and fired from the hip in one smooth,

153

lightning-quick motion.

The bullet smashed Clay backward, as if a giant fist had punched him in the chest. Mouth agape, wide-eyed in shocked disbelief, he staggered on wobbly legs he could no longer feel, and then . . . collapsed on the dirt.

The single gunshot faded.

The desert became deafeningly quiet.

No one moved. They scarcely breathed.

Finally, Drifter cautiously leaned over the body.

Clay didn't move. Blood welled from the bullet hole over his weakening heart, slowly but surely reddening his expensive gray velvet vest. His ice-blue eyes rolled up into his head. His long golden curls hung limply about his girlishly handsome face. His cruel smile disappeared as his lips twitched in agony. . . .

Drifter watched him fixedly, still not convinced that Clay was finished.

Stadtlander wasn't convinced either. Stunned that Clay had been beaten to the draw, he stared in disbelief at the dying gunman, as if expecting him to get up and shoot Drifter.

But Clay was done. He gave a final shudder, stiffened, and was still.

His death brought a rousing cheer from the townspeople lining the barricade.

It also made the mounted gunmen wonder if they were backing the wrong man. They exchanged worried looks. Then, as if in silent agreement, they all looked at Stadtlander. What they saw was troubling. Suddenly the invincible, once all-powerful rancher looked vulnerable. Worse, the farmers and townspeople that he'd assured them wouldn't put up much of a fight, showed no sign of backing down.

It was all the concerned gunmen needed. They again swapped worried looks. Then, as one, they decided that no amount of money was worth dying for, and without giving Stadtlander any warning, they spun their horses around and rode off into the darkening desert.

Their desertion caught Stadtlander by surprise. Then his shock turned to rage, and he started after them, waving his arms, shouting, ordering them to come back. But it was useless. They ignored him and kept riding.

Finally, he had no choice but to give up and return to his horse. It was a bitter defeat. And though outwardly he still retained his defiance, losing face in front of the farmers and townspeople was a shattering blow to his ego, and he had to force himself to confront Drifter.

'Go ahead, Longley,' he snarled. 'Start crowing!'

Drifter eyed him coldly. Though his expression never showed his inner feelings, he grudgingly had to admit to himself that Lars was right: he had grown tired of killing. Shooting even a murderous low-life like Clay Hudson had left a sour taste in his mouth. It was a feeling the tall gunfighter had never experienced before, though he had enough faith in himself to know that he'd eventually come to terms with it.

First, though, he knew it was up to him to make sure that Stadtlander never terrorized Santa Rosa again.

'This ain't about crowing,' he replied. 'This is about the future of my town.'

'*Your* town?' Stadtlander scoffed. 'That's a joke if I ever heard one. I mean, since when did a hard-core drifter like you ever call any town his?'

'Since as of right now,' Drifter said. 'What's more, Stillman, I'm giving you fair warning: unless you swear that you'll quit harassing the farmers and never – and I said, *never* – set foot in Santa Rosa again, then it'll be your turn to "face the consequences".'

Stadtlander, guessing the 'consequences' meant a bullet from Drifter's pistol, tried to bluff his way past his fear. 'Damn you to hell, Longley!'

'That's a nice sentiment,' Drifter said wryly, 'but you're too late. I was damned the first time I ever killed someone. And I ain't never doubted that I'm going to hell. But over the years I've learned to bury my conscience and live with that. 'Cause having no conscience, Stillman, means I can shoot a no-good, scum-sucking rat like you without the slightest remorse.'

Though Drifter spoke no louder than the faintly moaning wind, there was such menace in his voice that Stadtlander paled and took a backward step.

'Y-you wouldn't dare kill me,' he said. 'Not in front of all these witnesses. The law would surely hang you for murder!'

'Possibly,' Drifter admitted. 'But knowing I've rid Santa Rosa of the likes of you, hell, I figure it's worth it.'

Stadtlander stared into Drifter's pale gray eyes and saw death in them. *His* death. It was a chilling moment. And it had a strange effect on Stadtlander. As if realizing for the first time that Drifter truly intended to kill him, he suddenly seemed able to accept his fate – and once he'd accepted it, his demeanor changed. He straightened up, all fear gone, and glared defiantly at Drifter.

'Fine,' he snarled. 'You want to shoot me, Quint, go ahead. Pull that trigger. I mean it,' he added when Drifter didn't respond. 'Shoot me! Go on, damn you! Jerk that trigger and get it over with. Hell, truth is, you'll be doing me a favor. Ever since you killed my boy, I got nothing to live for, anyway.'

It was a Stadtlander that Drifter had never thought existed. He wondered for a moment if the rancher was bluffing. Then deciding he wasn't, Drifter holstered his pistol, saying: 'Sorry, Stillman, I can't oblige you.'

'Why in hell not?'

' 'Cause this ain't your day for dying.'

'What're you talking about?'

'You just gave me an idea.'

'Like, what?'

'You say you got nothing to live for? OK, I reckon that includes the Double-S as well as your son. So, here's my idea: you put all your holdings – ranch, land, cattle – up for sale, and leave this valley within one week. I don't care where you go. Just so you're gone. Permanently. Got it?'

Stadtlander nodded, but didn't say anything.

'Maybe you can start over someplace else,' Drifter continued, 'somewhere you won't be reminded of Slade every time you turn around, I don't know. That's for you to decide. But keep this in mind. Your leaving is the one and only reason I ain't pulling this trigger. And if I find out that you're still around when the week is up, I'll come a-gunning for you, and I won't let up till you're dead! Is that clear?'

'Clear.'

'Fair enough. Then jump on your horse and ride out of here. Now!'

Stadtlander had sense enough not to argue. Quickly mounting his stallion, he dug in his spurs and galloped off in the direction of his ranch.

A huge rousing cheer came from the farmers and townspeople. They joyfully hugged each other, and danced around like Fourth of July revelers.

Lars elbowed his way through the elated crowd and joined Drifter.

'Good work, bucko!'

'We'll see,' Drifter said, somewhat pessimistically. 'Only time will tell.'

'Sure,' Lars agreed. 'Listen,' he then said in a fatherly tone, 'we all know that having Stadtlander gone won't make up for the years of pain and hardship he's caused everyone in Santa Rosa. But it's sure a start in the right direction. What's more, bucko, you did the right thing.'

'By letting the bastard go, you mean?'

'Yeah – if for no other reason than it means you don't have to add another notch on your gun butt – something that's been bothering you of late, remember?'

If Drifter heard him, he didn't show it. He was uneasily watching the farmers and townspeople happily whooping it up.

Lars, noticing how worried Drifter looked, guessed what was troubling him. He chuckled and said:

158

'Reckon it's time you rode out of here, Quint.'

'What?'

'Get moving. Now! Before all them nice folks realize it's you they got to thank for getting rid of Stadtlander, and come rushing over here to carry you around on their shoulders!'

The thought almost panicked Drifter.

'Fair enough,' he said, relieved that he wouldn't have to endure everyone's gratitude. 'I'll see you around, *compadre.*'

'Count on it, bucko.'

The two men shook hands with a deep-rooted fondness that only exists between close, trusting friends.

Then Drifter gave Lars a throwaway salute and hurried off in the direction of the livery stable to saddle up the sorrel.